THE LUST LIST: MILES RIOT

BROKEN STRINGS

MIRA BAILEE

NoMi Press

Euphoria Publishing
NoMi Press
www.euphoriapublishing.com

Publisher's Note: This is a work of fiction. Names, characters, places, and incidents are a product of the author's imagination, and any resemblance to actual people, living or dead, or to businesses, companies, events, institutions, or locales is completely coincidental.

ISBN-13: 978-0692618851
ISBN-10: 0692618856

Printed in the United States of America

Dedicated to everyone

who's leaped out of their comfort zone

and found an adventure on the other side.

Chapter One

Miles

Let me tell you what really pisses me off. Just when you think you've got something really good going for you, bam! Your overdramatic, nosy sister has to ruin it all by announcing your girlfriend might just be using you to make money from some shitty tabloid. I shouldn't even bother calling her my girlfriend. Surprising her with that song yesterday went better than expected. Abby

Clarke—the sweet and sexy music journalist—had jumped me with more intensity and passion than any experienced groupie. The same girl who said she hated my music was singing a different tune when I was thrusting in and out of her. By this morning, I truly felt like she could be the woman I woke up to every day...at least for a while.

But just my luck. It was probably all a lie. I wasn't sure what to do after Kennedy showed me Abby's email from *ScandalLust*. It was clear as day—they were offering her fifty grand to leak any secrets she could dig up on us. And god knows we all have secrets.

Pacing up and down the hallway of the hotel, I dodge the bright Arizona sun sending cheery streams of light across the carpet. Today was supposed to be promising. Now it's all gone to hell. I do an about face, turning away from the window, and stomp back over to my manager's door. I need to talk to him, maybe even fire him. He's the one who invited Abby onto this tour. What's a reporter—a small town, Southern reporter who hates wild rock bands—doing on a national tour with us anyway? Eddie said she was here to write an article that'll help us get signed. Well, guess what Eddie? Your plan backfired.

I pound my fist against the door three times. Too impatient to wait for him, I knock two more times.

"Holy shit, I'm coming. Just wait," I hear from inside.

I hear the lock being twisted and the door opens up. It's dark in his room.

"The fuck, Miles?" Eddie runs a hand through his hair. He's in his boxers and he keeps his voice low. "I was sleeping."

"We need to talk."

"Later," he says, but I push past him and walk into his room. "I said *later*, Miles. You need to go."

I spot movement in the bed as a woman rolls over. She spots me and her eyes light up.

"Miles Riot," she says, sitting up in the bed, holding the sheet over her, assumedly, naked body. "Good morning."

I turn back to Eddie, crossing my arms over my chest.

"Come on, man," Eddie pleads, his voice barely above a whisper. "I'm about to be busy here, if you know what I mean."

"I'm not leaving until we talk." I walk over to an armchair and collapse into it. "Be as busy as you like. I'll wait."

Eddie looks over at his no-name friend as though he's really considering banging her right in front of me. Then he looks back at me, his eyes narrowed. "I thought you were the nice one."

"And I thought you were married."

Checkmate, Eddie. He looks defeated as he rummages in his suitcase for some pants. "We're going to have to cut this short," he tells the woman in his bed. "Business calls."

The woman gets up out of bed, her eyes more focused on me than Eddie. A smile teases at the corner of her lips as she drops the sheet. Yep, she's definitely naked. Her dark, chocolaty skin is hairless, and I imagine she spends a lot of time in a Pilates class. I'd be impressed with Eddie if blatantly cheating on his wife didn't make him an instant sleaze. I avert my eyes from the woman as she gets dressed. Two days ago, sure, I would've watched. A week ago, I would've seduced her into my own room. But now that Abby's in the picture, I'm not interested. She does something for me no other woman has been able to accomplish. She challenges me. She's authentic and doesn't care that we're total opposites. She likes it quiet and calm. I'm a fucking rock star. She's sweet and rational. I'm impulsive and make stupid decisions. Every second with her makes me want more.

And just thinking about her brings back all my anger. It could all be an act, and if so, Abby's the greatest liar of them all.

Eddie's friend waltzes past me, that seductive smile still on her face as she stares me down. She's just another woman using people to get what she wants. But I'm no different, am I? I was doing the same shit earlier this week, so why does it suddenly bother me now?

The sound of the door shutting behind her confirms I've got Eddie alone now.

"Fuck you very much, Miles," he says with synthetic anger. We'll be in Dallas sometime tonight, and Eddie's far from being a hideous dude, so he can pick up his antics again later.

"How's your wife, Eddie?"

"Probably banging every guy in the neighborhood."

"So you're having a contest to see who can betray who the most?"

"Whoa." Eddie holds his hands up to surrender and sits down in the other armchair across from me. "When did you suddenly become Mr. Monogamy?"

I shake my head. "Forget it. We have to talk about Abby."

"Is she the one who's got your panties all in a bunch?"

"I'm being serious, Eddie. Kennedy found something on her computer. She might be working with the tabloids. *ScandalLust* to be exact, which, last time I checked, is the worst of them all."

He sits there quietly, like he's contemplating something.

I continue, "We have to send her back to L.A., right?" Why's that even a question? She could ruin us. But even knowing that, I don't want her gone. I take a deep breath. "She's got to go." Maybe after we get signed, I'll be able to see her again.

"She's not going anywhere." Eddie sits up straighter, resting his elbows on his knees. He holds his head in his hands for a second, tugging at his hair. He's probably still angry I cock blocked him.

"Did you not hear me? *ScandalLust* contacted her. They're working out deals. They want secrets, and you know more than anyone, we can't let secrets get out."

He looks back up at me, this time a smile on his face. Call me confused. "Don't you think I know that? Damn, man. You've got to give me more credit than that. When I started booking this tour, I knew the media would butt in. We had to be one step ahead. They uncover scandals through their own detective work, right? Bullshit. I leak the rumors straight to them. The lies they publish about you guys? Those are hand selected by yours truly."

"That's fucked up. Even if they aren't true, selling them dirt on us? That's low."

"Not 'us', Miles. *Them.* Your bandmates. If they flood their trash rags with generic made up stories about the others, it keeps you in the shadows. The secrets remain buried. But they're still digging, so I found Abby. Sweet, little Southern Abby. A small town, impressionable girl who could be heavily influenced by some hot rock stars. I picked her out intentionally to work in our favor. To publish a sparkling article about you all to make you more appealing, no matter what *Scandal*Sluts says."

"And that's obviously backfired, don't you think? She's going to go from helping us to ruining us—"

"They may be contacting her," he interjects, "but I'll bet you right now she won't follow through. I'm fantastic at gambling. I wouldn't suggest taking that bet." He winks. But then he gets serious again. "Look, she's not going to fuck you over. Her boss is an old friend of mine, and Jonathan even said she's not the type to throw around slander. She's got ethics. She holds high standards. She won't take *ScandalLust's* bait."

"You're certain of that?"

"More than certain. Especially when you can help make sure of it. Just get her to fall for you. Or maybe even Nate. Ladies seem to love him. Or if she's into the shaved head thing, then Dax. Maybe we'll all luck out, and she's into Kennedy. That would be hot."

My stomach turns at the thought. "That's my sister, asshole."

"Right. Sorry. Whoever can lure her in, one of you needs to make sure she falls for him. Then they have to make sure she stays interested. She's already a good journalist. Just make her a faithful girlfriend, and you'll have nothing to worry about."

My manager...talking about being faithful. It's sort of sick. But is he on to something? He has no idea what happened between me and Abby. He doesn't know that her falling for me is taking me right down with her. But if she needs to have feelings for one of us in order for Eddie's plan to work? Consider that one done.

I leave his room feeling that much more conflicted. I like the woman. It's been so long since I truly felt interest in someone romantically, wanting something more than just a quick lay. But now, to follow through with my own feelings, am I doing it for me or for the band? If it's for the well-being of the band—

to make sure we stay in a positive spotlight, then what happens if Abby finds out I'm using her?

And if it's for me, because there is something between us worth exploring...*then* what?

Chapter Two

Abby

So many explanations are running through my mind. He went out for coffee. He woke up and realized he's not interested in me at all. He's just hanging out with the band in the living room of our suite. He's shacked up in another room with some random woman.

I shake my head. *Don't act like a neurotic fool.* Standing in the shower, letting the hot water wake me up from an exhausting, exhilarating night, I'm thinking of only one thing.

Why was Miles gone when I woke up?

Last night couldn't have been a one-night stand. In my short time knowing this band, I'd seen how Miles acts. He'd pick up girls without much thought. It would be effortless because they were already half-naked and throwing themselves at him. They hardly had to speak to each other, and by morning, they were both content with throwing each other away in favor of their next adventure.

But it was different last night. He'd gone out of his way to buy an acoustic guitar and write me a song. He'd used it to prove his feelings were authentic. And after we had sex in the warm-up room backstage at the concert hall, we'd come back here and done it again. And again.

He could've snuck out in the night, returning to his own room, but I'd woken up before the sun, slightly disoriented as I placed where I was and who I was with. As the sleep dissipated to wakefulness, the moonlight filtered through my room, tossing a cool glow over Miles. Both of us naked in bed, wrapped around each other. His arm held me tight against him, my head against his chest. Even in his sleep, his closeness, his content breathing, it proved it to me.

It was no one-night stand.

I shut off the water and step out of the shower. A new thrill is coursing through me this morning. There's something about Miles—I don't care how loud his music is or how troubled he might seem on the outside. There's so much more to him, and I want to know it.

Unfortunately, *ScandalLust* wants to know it too.

I can't throw the band under the bus now. Not when something new and great could be happening between me and their guitarist. But I want to know the truth for myself. It's personal now. If the rumors *ScandalLust* pointed out are true, then I think I have a right to know what I'm getting myself into. But I can't just ask them. If I'm asking the same questions *ScandalLust* is asking, they'll figure out pretty fast there's a connection. And if they think I'm working with *Scandal-Lust*, they'll never see me as anything less than a liar—just another paparazzi rat.

But that's the least of my worries. Standing in the bathroom naked, I dry myself, leaning forward to rub the towel through my blond hair. I love the red and black ends now. I'm tempted to thank Kennedy for bringing out my inner spunkiness. After all, it led to last night. I laugh out loud in the empty bathroom. Now, I'm just acting like a crazed schoolgirl, excited about her new boyfriend.

Miles isn't my boyfriend though. Not yet, at least. But maybe—

There's a knock on the door and I sling the towel around myself, covering my body the best it can. Who's looking for me? Or does someone think this is Miles's room, and they're looking for *him*?

No one saw us last night. No one knows we stayed in the same room. Having a couple more days on tour with these guys, I'd like to keep it that way. I don't want things to get weird.

Another knock, and I hesitate as I walk to the door. *Own it, Abby!* I hold my head high and open the door, expecting to have to do some explaining.

But it's Miles.

"Hi," I say, my smile giving away my obvious joy of seeing him. "You didn't have to knock—"

I barely get the last word out when his mouth is on mine. He crushes his body against me, forcing me back a couple feet. Once we're out of the way, he slams the door behind him while he keeps kissing me, his warm tongue stroking mine as his hands grip the top edges of the towel.

I sink into his kiss, stepping back until my legs hit the side of the bed. I lean into the bed, letting Miles push me further back. The towel betrays me, falling open and giving Miles a full display of my naked, damp body. He takes in a deep breath.

"You smell amazing," he says.

Then his mouth finds me again, nibbling at my thighs as he moves up higher. My back arches involuntarily as he kisses the folds of my sex, teasing me, only lingering a second before he's gone again. In the mere seconds since he's walked in, I find my whole body aching for him. It's like we never stopped last night, and I'm ready to beg him to be inside me again.

Miles's hands lead their way up my sides, finding my breasts and squeezing firmly. He twists at my nipples as he climbs on top of me. I feel that much more vulnerable with him fully clothed and me completely exposed. It feels like he's dominating me, and I love it.

When he reaches my lips, I can't help but smile. He reciprocates with his own mischievous grin.

"Good morning," he tells me now.

"The best kind of morning."

After another long kiss, he rolls away from me, holding my hips as he does and pulling me onto him. The textures of his shirt and jeans tease my sensitive skin as I hover over his mouth.

It's one of those moments when I want to say something extra sexy. Something to push him over the edge and make him want to claim me hard and fast.

But words aren't coming to me, so instead, I kiss him softly along his jaw, down to his neck. I feel his pulse pounding against my lips. I graze my teeth along his neck and hear him groan. *Good.* Then I bite a little harder and feel his fingers dig into the skin at my waist. *Even better.* I move up to his ear, and when I bite his earlobe, I moan softly, and that seems to do the trick. He moves us both up to standing, his eyes fiercely watching me as he gives me a soft shove into the wall. He rips his shirt over his head, his chest heaving with every inhale. I follow his hands as he

moves to his jeans and admire the hard outline of his excited cock. He ditches the rest of
his clothes in one fell swoop and comes at me
again. My heart races, wanting him to take
me. Dominate me. Make me his.

He grabs my wrists and pulls my arms up
over my head, locking them in place against
the wall with one of his hands. With the other, his fingers trail down the side of my face,
tracing their way down to my chin, where he
clutches my jaw. He steps forward, his whole
body pressed against mine now, and turns my
head to the side. His teeth find my neck in re-
taliation, and I sigh with ecstasy.

"You like that?" His voice is low and rough,
the sound of it sending chills down my spine.

"I want more."

His hands drop away from me, freeing my
arms, as he runs his fingers down my breasts,
my belly, my hips. Each hand finds their way
to my thighs, pulling my legs apart, giving
room for his hard length to bury itself against

my cleft. He's so close to being in me, my muscles throb for him.

"What do you want more of?" he asks. So considerate when every touch is like torturous bliss.

"I want whatever you want." This time my wide eyes meet his and I try to look as sweet and innocent as possible. "Surprise me."

This nice, well-mannered Southern girl wants boundaries to be pushed. I don't want to make love right now. I want Miles Riot to fuck me however he likes it best. I want to see what he can really be like.

And he takes my offer seriously. He walks away from me without a word, and at first I'm scared. Did I just disappoint him? But he goes to his suitcase on the other side of the room and gets out a condom. When he turns back to me, he's completely ready.

"Come here," he says, but I must not move fast enough. "Now."

The demand sends fire through my body. Yes, this is what I want from him right now. I want things the Miles way.

As soon as I'm close enough, he reaches out and grabs a fistful of my hair, clutching it as he pulls me into him. He's breathing fast and rough as his mouth collides with mine.

The enormous window overlooking the vast stretch of desert and mountains makes for a sexy backdrop. The sunlight has us both illuminated, two naked bodies with nothing to hide—no inhibitions.

He spins me around so my back is to the window, and then he pushes me against it. The cold glass is shocking until the heat of my own body warms it, but even more shock-ing is the image in my imagination. If anyone happened to walk by the building and look up to this exact window twenty-three floors up, they'd see my shoulders and ass smashed against the glass. They'd see my blond hair tangled around Miles's hand. They'd see his free arm grip my right thigh as he pulls it up, urging me to wrap my leg around his waist.

Damn, what a view.

Back in the room though, it feels like the temperature has been turned up to scalding. It's hard to breathe as my heart pounds with anticipation. As soon as my leg is secure around him, my balance depends on his strong arms now, and as soon as we both know I'm angled just right, he plunges himself into me and we both cry out from how good it feels. My hands yearn to grab something. I claw my nails up his back as he thrusts into me deep and fast. My fingers entangle themselves into his messy hair, and I tug gently.

"Don't be nice about it," he tells me, so I pull harder, and he laughs. "That's my girl."

He pulls out slowly only to ram into me even harder. My moans can't be quieted now. I hold on tight to the back of his neck, holding myself in place as I pull my supporting leg up and around him. His hands move down to my ass to hold me up, and now I'm all his.

Up against this hotel window, where anyone could see if they're observant enough, I'm having the ride of my life. Each thrust makes me want more. Our bodies coated in a sheen of sweat, neither one of us able to breathe steadily, I can feel all the muscles in me tightening. The need for release can be felt all the way to my toes.

"Harder," I plead, and he intensifies his force, almost sending me over the edge.

The glass behind me shakes each time we hit it, a steady pounding that keeps pace with my own trembling. I feel Miles tensing more inside me and know he's feeling the same way. This feels too good to stop, but we're both reaching a breaking point.

"Come with me," Miles demands, no sense of pleading in his voice.

It's enough to make me come unbound, and I feel my body give in to the orgasm. I cry out and feel Miles pulsating in me. He lets out a growl as he comes inside me, but he keeps thrusting, keeps forcing me to feel every wave of intensity long after I think I can stand it. I need to come down. It's too much. My entire body screams as another orgasm hits. My moans are turning to whimpers and stuck in his grip, nowhere to go, he asks me if I want more.

No. No. It's too much. I need to lie down. I need to breathe. I need my body to settle. "Keep going."

He's moving slower now, knowing my sensitive muscles are fighting to push him out of me. I can feel every inch of him massaging me. My body shakes with adrenaline and exhaustion, but I concentrate on the way he feels in me. How it sends an earthquake to my core with every movement. I bury my head into his neck, breathing in his musky scent, as I come one last time.

"Oh god. Oh. Miles."

"I like the sound of that."

He holds me to him a moment longer before carrying me to the bed. We both collapse in a daze.

"You're shaking," he says.

I sigh, barely able to speak. "Your fault," I say with a satisfied smile on my face.

He pulls a thin sheet over us and lays closer to me. Our legs are tangled together, my hands are cupped in his. I look up at him and watch him watching me. When our eyes meet he kisses me, much gentler than any of his actions since he walked into this room, but when he pulls away, there's a different look on his face.

He looks troubled.

"You okay?" I ask him. Now's not the time to be second-guessing us, Miles. At least wait until the post-sex high wears off.

Just as he starts to answer, the door bursts open, and Nate walks in.

"If you two are finished, we have to get to Dallas." He does an about face and leaves without waiting for a response.

I should be embarrassed being caught in the act, right? I should feel some shame. But I don't. I don't care at all. Instead, I erupt into a fit of giggles. The laughter's contagious and Miles joins in, the dark look long gone from his eyes as he pulls me into a hug and kisses my forehead.

Guess there's no hiding this from the others now.

Chapter Three

Abby

If Nate walking in on us was awkward...riding on a tour bus when you're sleeping with the guitarist is, well, I'm not sure there's even a name for how I've felt on the road today. At first, I thought it would be fine. Everyone knows anyway, so how much weirder can it get? Turns out, a whole lot.

Let's start with walking onto the bus. It's a narrow space, and up to that point, I'd claimed a chair off to the side so I could work without being in the middle of things. Now, I had to choose. Should I keep to myself? Should I hang out with everyone? I didn't want to be some presumptuous girlfriend, but I didn't want them thinking I was antisocial or rude.

I also wanted to avoid Kennedy. So far, she hadn't even made eye contact, but it was only a matter of time before she made her feelings known. She'd remind me I was here for my job, and she'd be right. I am still here professionally, and I do have to find time to get this article written. I figured bus time was the best time, so that was my easy solution. I spent hours working through all the ways I could spin my article and even got through the full first draft. By that point, the sun had long since disappeared beyond the horizon, and the band was nearly passed out from playing games with shot glasses. That's when it dawned on me...the bunks. Sure, there's a bed in the back, but there was no way I was up for sharing a mattress with the others and all their groupies. So, bunk it was. That put Miles and I foot-to-foot when we're both in there, a six-inch barrier between our closest body parts. Two of us definitely couldn't squeeze into one bunk, and so it felt very 1950s to say goodnight and climb into our separate bed. Mental note: tour buses and dating don't go hand-in-hand.

*

The next morning, I'm woken up by soft, warm lips on my own. His scent overtakes me, and before I open my eyes, I'm convinced we're in the hotel room again after a long, eventful night together. But when I wake up, I'm back in my bunk with Miles standing next to the open curtain. I get a vision of Prince Charming awakening his princess after she's been cast under a spell. I hold off the laugh. Rock star Miles wouldn't find it as amusing.

"You're turning into one of us, sleeping this late." He rests his arms against the edge of my mattress, leaning in to talk to me quietly. This is the best you can get when it comes to privacy on this bus. He kisses my bare shoulder and tugs the blanket away. "You get those panties off, I can give you a really special morning kiss."

My body shivers from the offer, but my Prince Charming vision just got really dirty. "And how many people would be sitting five feet away watching?"

"Don't mind them."

I laugh. He's out of his mind though. "We're in Dallas now, right?"

"Yep. We're in your territory now." He winks.

He doesn't realize home is still an hour drive and all we have is this bus. But it does feel good to be in a familiar area. I haven't been back since last Christmas. "Maybe I can take you sightseeing." I immediately want to take the words back. Miles? Sightseeing like a tourist?

"Sounds good. But first we have a photo shoot with Max Music Magazine."

"Hmm. The triple M. Lydian Magazine's competition," I joke.

"You can come along. Tell them how to do their job right."

"I think I'll stay behind. The faster I get this article done, the faster I'm no longer a journalist following you on tour. I can just be your—" I stop myself. I can throw the girl-friend term around in my head, but I'm not about to make Miles think I'm tying him down. Who knows what this guy thinks of commitment?

That dark look flashes across his face again, and I know I didn't stop myself fast enough. I've got to be careful or I'll scare him off.

"Get your work done." He kisses me again, but it's quicker and much less suggestive than when he woke me up. "I'll see you soon."

I wait until everyone leaves to get up. After taking a quick shower and getting dressed in the cramped bathroom, I sit down with my laptop.

I open the article to start the second draft. I went the simple route and wrote about my experiences on tour while feeling completely out of place. I added some humor into it, but it's mostly just a typical opinion piece. It's safe. It gets the job done. Jonathan will be content, and my job should be safe.

But I'm not in the mood to work. I procrastinate online and then decide to call and check in with Dee.

"Hello," says in a sleepy voice, and I remember it's earlier in the morning in California.

"I'm so sorry. Did I wake you up?"

"No. I was up. Just not awake yet." I hear my coffee grinder in the background. "Chord says hi."

My golden retriever is my family in L.A., and I'm amazed how much I feel homesick without him. "Give him a good belly scratch for me."

"Uh huh. Enough with the small talk. When were you going to tell me?"

Her voice is suddenly accusatory, but I don't know what she's talking about. "What do you mean?"

I multitask while I talk, scanning over online articles on Lydian's site and checking my work emails. There's another one from *ScandalLust* that's short and sweet.

Hello again Ms. Clarke,

We're very interested in meeting with you to discuss our offer. Let us know the time and location, and we'll accommodate.

Polly Hemsworth

ScandalLust

"*ScandalLust*," Dee says, as if she's looking over my shoulder. "It's so wrong that they knew before me."

"I don't know what you're..." I trail off, opening a new search page in my browser. I can look this up myself. On the home page of

ScandalLust, they feature their top stories. I scroll down past this morning's big discoveries (a.k.a. Big lies). About two-thirds of the way down, I almost scroll past it. But I freeze and scroll back up. It's a dark picture, a little blurry. Two people holding hands, sneaking away together. The clearest part of the photo is Miles's face. And only someone who knows me would recognize the woman he's with.

"You hooked up with the guitarist, didn't you?" There's no denying the thrill in her voice.

I can't lie. "You could say that."

She squeals, and I hear Chord bark in the background. "I knew it! I knew you wouldn't be able to resist that giant hunk of sexy. Tell me. How was he?"

"I'm sorry. You'll have to consult with my agent if you want an interview." I throw her the same excuse I've heard countless times from singers.

"Ok...off the record then?"

"Off the record, I'm more confused than ever."

"Confused." She pauses. "But you've had sex before. Right?"

"Not about that," I yell at her. Then I lower my voice as though anyone's around to hear. The band won't be back for a few hours, easily. "*ScandalLust* is trying to get me to leak information to them."

"What's confusing about that? It's your story, not theirs. Why would you share details that you can run exclusively?"

"It comes with an enormous incentive. To the tune of fifty grand."

"Shit." That's all she says. I could use more of a response. "But that's still ridiculous. You're better than that."

"I know. I just woke up with this revelation. The rumors they're wanting me to look into...aren't really secrets anyway. They're more like...stupid generalizations people would expect of a rock band—just a little more legally problematic." As I talk, I do a general search for Tempest Ultra. Not much comes back, and I remember their name change. I search for Vitriol instead. "There's nobody credible reporting on things like drug scandals and illegal activities. It's all tabloid b.s. So...couldn't I take advantage of *Scandal-Lust* by feeding them the things that'll be seen as lies anyway? And in return, I make major cash?"

"And possibly screw over the guy you're screwing."

I laugh, but it's really not funny. "No. I'd keep him out of it." I stand up and survey the bus. No way am I going to search through the band's things, but if there's anything out in the open, then it's not a big deal to accidentally see it, right? My heart pounds as I walk to the back room where Kennedy stayed last night. "They smoke pot openly, so letting *ScandalLust* exaggerate and say they sell it too is barely newsworthy. And with Kennedy, they want to report on how she uses sex to make extra cash." Inside the bedroom, I quickly scan the space, my heart pounding like someone's going to walk in behind me. The room's a mess, but if you want to know what Kennedy thinks about sex, she's got little to hide. A tiny piece of lingerie lays on the bed. It's black and made of fake leather. Not your ordinary pajamas. "If it's true at all, Devon Stone would've gotten involved."

"So why not just smile and nod and let them report whatever they want?"

"Because they want some sort of proof. They want to be able to say they got the inside scoop, and I'll need to give them tangible evidence before they hand that check over." Just saying it makes me feel dirty. This is wrong.

I glance over my shoulder again, but shake it off. They're at a photo shoot. I have time, but what am I doing? I need to decide. Either take the plunge, find some dirt, and let Polly Hemsworth sign that check, or turn around, leave this room, and forget about it.

I know which is right, but the thrill of being a detective is teasing me at the same time. At the nightstand next to the bed, I reach down and open the top drawer. Just a quick peek. I won't touch anything.

Condoms, a book, a silky bag. Judging buy the outline of what's inside that bag, I can clearly see it's a sex toy. Yeah, Kennedy likes her sex, but it doesn't mean she's selling her body for it. She doesn't need the money, but as I look around, I'm getting the sense she wasn't in here pleasing herself alone recently. The bed's a ruffled mess, a man's black undershirt lies crumpled on the floor, and a torn condom wrapper peeks out from underneath Kennedy's dominatrix-style lingerie.

Either Devon Stone came back to visit or Kennedy's cheating on him.

"You still there?" Dee asks.

"Yeah." I make sure the nightstand drawer is closed and I quickly leave the room. "You know. I don't think I'll find anything anyway. These guys really aren't that scandalous."

My voice is hardly convincing.

"Keep your eye out. You might be on to something. If it's not news anyway, but you can sell it to *ScandalLust* as the inside scoop, you really could make that fifty grand without doing any damage."

That's not what I was looking for. I need her to talk me out of it, tell me it's a waste of time, not encourage me.

After we hang up, I return to my laptop, closing it and putting it back in my bunk. When I turn around, I notice the curtain of Nate's bunk is wide open. I look at Dax's. It's closed.

I refuse to snoop. Opening a single drawer in Kennedy's room has already filled me with guilt, so I won't look inside Dax's bunk. But Nate's. I'm not sneaking around by merely taking a couple steps forward and looking at what's in front of me.

A messy bed, a closed duffel bag, and a small tray holding a half-smoked joint.

See what I mean? Not newsworthy at all. And nothing that lends any truth to the stories of them dealing drugs or diving into the sex industry. That settles it then. *Scandal-Lust* will have to look elsewhere.

Feeling the growing need to get off this bus and clear my head, I grab my shoes, put them on, and start toward the bus door.

But I stop short. The curtain to Miles's bunk is half open. Is this some evil joke from the universe? I genuinely like Miles. There could be something between us, and the last thing I want to do is introduce any sort of sneaking around into our relationship. Honesty is key, and of all the things I know I don't know about him, I'd rather him tell me himself. So I'm making the choice not to look in the bunk. I'm confident I wouldn't find anything anyway.

But my heart tugs at me. I want to be near him. As I stand next to his bunk, I put my hand on the corner of his pillow and picture the way he looks when he's asleep next to me—content, untroubled. How did the two of us end up at this place? We're so...incompatible. I smile at the thought of "opposites attract" actually being true. Maybe they don't just attract. They collide at the force of two steam trains.

"Miss me?"

I nearly scream as I spin to the door and see Miles stepping onto the bus. He looks immaculate, dressed in a black button down shirt and ripped jeans, his hair styled to look just the right amount of disheveled. I tell myself to shut my gaping mouth and hold back the urge to drool.

"You're back early." It's all I can think to say. How weird is it to find the woman you're sleeping with staring at your pillow? Then again, it's a bus. An enclosed space. Maybe I don't look as crazy as I feel.

"They did group shots first. Then I made them do my solo series before Ken's so I wouldn't have to wait through all her prima donna bullshit."

"Smart," I say. "I was just standing here thinking..."

"About what you want to do to me?" A sly smile stretches across Miles's face as he walks closer to me, wrapping his arms around my waist. He pulls me into a kiss, and he tastes as good as he looks.

"More like what I want *you* to do to *me*."

He moves to my neck, kissing me, and before my eyes fall shut, something grabs my attention. On the wall of Miles's bunk is a bright, yellow sticky note. I wasn't paying attention before, but now that I've noticed it it's impossible not to see what it says. In dark red marker, the contrast is high enough someone could use it for an eye exam.

Friday @ 1:00

Frankie's Deli

Forget about it. So he has an appointment tomorrow afternoon. It doesn't mean he's the one hiding *ScandalLust*-worthy secrets. It's probably nothing.

"What's wrong?" Miles asks me.

"Nothing. We should get off this bus though. I'm starting to feel a little cabin-feverish."

He takes my hand and leads the way. "It's about time I took you out anyway."

Chapter Four

Miles

When I see that dark look cross Abby's face, Eddie's conversation plays back through my mind. Does she have any idea that she's part of a plan to keep the Tempest name clean? If she found out that part of the scheme involved making her fall for one of us, would she believe me if I said my feelings were real?

I'm not going to waste time worrying. Even if the truth came out, if she chose to believe anyone else other than me, then she'd be proving to me she wasn't the right woman after all.

"This is your turf. Where should we go?"

We get off the bus and start walking.

"My *turf*," she says, "is about one hundred miles away from here. This little town called Brenton."

"That's right. Small town girl. I can't imagine growing up someplace so...simple."

She laughs and takes my hand, interlocking her fingers with mine. It feels foreign at first—I've gotten accustomed to the lay-them-and-lose-them routine—but her skin feels soft and warm encased in my hand. I grip her fingers tighter, feeling the need to possess her. To claim her as mine. No, not as a piece of property. More like...like I *need her*. Horror sweeps through me, as I realize how attached I feel to this woman I hardly know, one who might be figuring out a way to break me.

"Where did you grow up?" she asks me. I get that instant urge to blow off her questions, but I remind myself this isn't an interview.

"L.A. for about ten years. Then I was on the East Coast for a while before ending up right back in Cali." Considered a troubled child, I was bounced from one parent to the other. Meanwhile, Kennedy was the child prodigy who could do no wrong. She was just better at hiding her indiscretions. Funny how things turned out. Now she's the drama queen I'm always bailing out of trouble.

"Where do you consider home to be?"

"I'll let you know when I figure it out."

"Oh, come on." Abby pushes herself into me playfully. "There's got to be one place where you feel perfectly at ease. Where you go for holidays or where you wish you were when you're having a rough time or are sick. I mean—"

"No." I cut her off. She really doesn't get it. "*You* may have that. But trust me, I don't."

Her face goes serious and sadness fills her eyes. "Sorry. I just thought you were—"

"Being a hard ass and taking things for granted? Nah. I'm a realist when it comes to life. But don't pity me. I'm doing exactly what I want. I'm exactly where I want to be. You might even call me happy."

I drop her hand, and wrap my arm around her hips, pulling her closer to me. She stops walking and turns toward me, kissing me hard. It's a little unexpected, but the sweet taste of her tongue leaves me intoxicated and craving more.

She pulls away too soon. "I want to keep you that way."

I raise an eyebrow. "Huh?"

"Happy." She smiles and kisses me one more time, hooking her fingers into the belt loops on my jeans and tugging my hips closer to hers.

The slamming of a car door interrupts the moment, and I look up in time to see three dudes from *ScandalLust* hurrying over with their cameras.

"Oh, for fuck's sake." I take Abby's hand and lead her past them, but it's obvious they're here for me as they follow close behind.

Another thought runs through my mind. How's Abby reacting? I mean, if she's working with these guys, the guilt could be plastered on her face. I look over, but I can't read her body language. She's tense, walking fast to keep up with me. Her eyes are focused forward and the only thing I sense from her is fear.

Is she scared of interacting with the paparazzi and getting caught up in celebrity drama? Or is she scared that I'll find out she's partnering up with the enemy?

"How can we lose these guys?" she asks.

I don't know this area, but I do know there were a couple security guards at the entrance to Studio 99 where the band's finishing up this morning's photo shoot. But this is a good chance to see where Abby's alliance lies.

"It's no big deal. They're just going to snap bad photos of us walking, get bored, and go away."

"I hate being near them." Is it confession time? "They're intrusive and don't take no for an answer."

I don't know if she's referring to the way they act with celebrities or how they've been acting with her. Apparently, I'm not getting any sort of reassurance from this today.

At the next block, we make a left. "Studio 99 is right down here. We can hide out there."

She squeezes my hand. "Thanks. Sorry, I'm not used to this sort of attention."

"I don't think there's any getting used to it."

We reach the big warehouse and rush in. One of the guards recognizes me from earlier and nods, letting us walk straight in. The paps try to follow behind, but both guards walk them back out the front doors and tell them to get lost.

I watch Abby relax and then look around. "Where are we?"

"Come here." I take her back to the large studio, and we find Nate and Dax hanging around a food table while Kennedy's in the middle of her shoot."

"You guys done here?" I ask them.

They both look irritated. Nate lets out a huff. "Not even fucking close. Your sister's being a diva."

"A fucking camera hog," Dax throws in.

Abby drops her purse on the table and we walk over to Gerard, the photographer. A woman is directing the shoot—Kirsty, if I remember her name right. Both of them seem energized and ready to go like they just got started. They had a 1965 Shelby Cobra con- vertible driven into the studio to use as our backdrop. The top down, the band photos were taken in all combinations of us inside and outside of the classic car—which, I have a feeling was set up by the Stones. I know Devon has an infatuation with antique sports cars. So now, they've got Kennedy sprawled across the seats as they take provocative photos of my sister. It's nauseating.

"You guys about done here? We've got shit to do before tonight's show." They don't need to know that "shit" is merely shots of bourbon and agreeing on a set list. I just don't want to see my little sister like this.

Gerard looks up from his camera and does a double take when he sees us. No, not us. Abby. He better not be some perv. One move on Abby, and that camera will be shoved right up his ass.

"I'm sorry. We didn't meet earlier," Kirsty says to Abby, walking over and shaking her hand. "I'm Kirsty."

"Abby," she says politely.

Kirsty looks from Abby to me and back to Abby. "You two make a very sexy couple."

Abby's cheeks turn red. No one's acknowledged the *couple* thing, not even us.

Reaching out and touching the tips of Abby's hair, Kirsty surveys her for a moment before asking, "Can we shoot you?"

Abby looks startled until she remembers we're at a photo shoot. "I'm not in the band."

"No. But we're trying to capture the personalities of each member in Tempest. I think you bring out another side to our friend Miles here."

Abby scrunches her forehead as though she's ready to call bullshit. "Two seconds of us standing here convinced you of that?"

"Hello," an irritated voice comes from behind. Kennedy must be losing her patience not having all the attention on her. "We were in the middle of my shoot, you guys. Maybe you can take your love connection elsewhere." She rolls her eyes and glares at me. The look says a million things. Mostly, *did you forget about what we talked about? She's going to fuck everything up.*

Unfortunately for her, I stopped listening to Kennedy's bitchy, manipulative looks long ago.

"I'll give you ten minutes. But then I want you to photograph the guys and let us get out of here."

Kirsty claps her hands in excitement and calls over a stylist who whisks Abby away. Kennedy is directed off the set, and a couple people from the crew rush over to follow Kirsty and Gerard's orders. They move some spotlights around, add a filter, and change the drop cloth in the back from white to black. Why am I allowing this? Of course, there's not much else to do while we wait for the paps to disappear, and at the same time, I like the idea of them taking hot photos of Abby.

You two make a very sexy couple.

Couple. What a surprising concept. That's not what I was looking for when I took on the challenge of getting Abby into bed with me. But something happened between our first introductions and that night backstage in

Tucson. I won't say I fell for her, but I haven't been interested in any one-night stands since.

This could be trouble.

And then that trouble walks back out of a dressing room. Abby's now dressed in leather pants and a white lacy corset top. The dark makeup around her eyes and blood red stain on her lips makes her look like a drop dead gorgeous pin-up girl I could bend across the hood of this car and fuck right now if there weren't a bunch of spectators. Fuck, even with people watching, I'd go for it.

She walks over to me, and I move in to kiss her, wanting the heat of her mouth.

"No, no, no!" Kirsty stops me. "We can't mess up that makeup. You only gave us ten minutes."

"Let me ruin it, and I'll give you an hour."

Abby laughs.

"Save it for after, Romeo. That level of lust will look great in print." Kirsty moves us into place and tells us what to do while I struggle to focus on keeping myself off Abby. "All right, for this first set, Abby, you sit on the hood behind Miles. Miles, get between her legs."

You don't have to tell me twice. I step in between her leather-clad thighs, my face inches from hers.

"Turn around and face the camera, rock star."

These ten minutes are going to be the death of me.

"Okay, now Abby, sit up straighter and lean closer to Miles. Move to the side a little so we can see that sweet face."

I feel her moving behind me.

Kirsty continues, "Now reach up and bring each hand to the side of Miles's head, right where his hair is. Grab some of that hair, like you're going to tug on it."

Her hands obey, and as soon as she pulls my hair, I'm reminded of yesterday morning at the hotel, fucking her against the window. Wish these camera people had been outside to capture that beautiful image.

"Perfect, you two. Seriously, there's so much electricity in these photos, you could power this whole set on that alone."

A cheesy remark, but whatever. A few more minutes and Abby and I can get out of here. God knows what I'm going to do to her the second we find some privacy.

"Okay, for this next set, let's get in the car." Kirsty pulls me away from the clutches of Abby and pushes me into the driver's seat of the Shelby. "Come here, Abby. I'm going to need you to be a little flexible for this one."

She helps Abby into the car, this time straddling me *and* facing me, her knees bent and our legs pressed thigh-to-thigh. I'm growing harder by the second, and just looking at Abby feels like torture.

Kirsty steps away to see how we look from a distance.

I look at Abby, her eyes dark and intense. She's feeling it too. "After this—"

"Yes," is all she says, and we're on the same page.

She adjusts her positioning to get more comfortable—or to tease me.

"Abby, I want you to lean away, arching your back against the steering wheel ... good ... Now turn your head this way, chin up a little, and close your eyes ... Perfect. "

Perfect is right.

"Now Miles, I want you to pretend she's not even there."

Is she fucking serious? No way in hell is that possible. Look at her, like a goddess.

Kirsty keeps directing us. "Put your right hand on her left shoulder like she *is* the steering wheel and then look this way. I'd tell you guys to dig deep for all the sexuality you can muster, but it's clear that's not necessary. Give me that smoldering glare, Miles." The sound of the camera shutter is nonstop as they get their shot. "Perfect. Unbelievably perfect. These are so much better than your solo photos, and those were already flawless."

Get me out of this car and into Abby. The ten minutes I promised have to be up.

"Okay, can we get one more?" Kirsty asks.

"Where are we on time?"

She looks at her watch. "It's right at ten minutes. We can fit—"

"Time's up," I say. I grab Abby by the hips and lift her off me. I get out of the car and extend my hand to help her out. "Let's go."

Her eyes are wide and focused on only me. It's like everyone else has disappeared. As soon as I pull her to standing, I yank her toward me, my mouth finally meeting hers. I plunge my tongue past her lips to take in her sweet taste. My breath shudders as her hands claw into my back. I feel her fingers run up my spine, up my neck, and into my hair, while one of my hands finds her ass and pulls her into me even closer. My other hand grazes her jaw, and when we pull apart, I draw a line across her bottom lip with my thumb.

"God damn, Miles. These are even better," Kirsty says as Gerard shows her the preview screen on the back of his camera. Apparently, they just photographed this moment too.

The two of them scroll through the photos, eyes wide while Abby retrieves her purse. Every now and then, one of them says, "Wow" or "Look at that one."

"You should see this, Miles," Kirsty says, waving me over.

But one look at Abby, and I don't care about the photos. "I'm busy," I say and head toward the doors that exit out the back of the studio. Kennedy stands next to them, arms crossed.

She doesn't think she's going to stop me right now, does she?

"We need to talk." She takes a step closer, getting between us and the door. Her eyes are filled with fury.

I sidestep around her, shoving her shoulder as I pass. "No, we don't."

I push open the door as she yells behind us, "Nice show you two put on. I'm sure it'll work out great for us in the long run." Her voice trembles, and I can sense the warning she's trying to get across.

"What was that about?" Abby asks, but the moment the door closes behind us, I spin around and push her into it, kissing her again.

She stops suddenly and pushes away. "I just realized I'm not in my own clothes. I should go change."

I laugh. "My sister might be a pain in the ass, but the first thing she did when we got here was make them agree to let us keep the whole wardrobe. She doesn't like paying for clothes."

"So then why's she in a bad mood now?"

I don't know how to answer. I use my normal, canned response. "Because she's Kennedy."

Abby opens her mouth to push it further, but then her phone rings.

"Ignore it. Let's go back to the bus and—"

"Sorry, no. Not the bus. It's nice and all, but um...it's also used." She finds her phone and her eyes go bright. "It's my sister."

She answers, walking a few feet away to have her conversation. After she hangs up, she comes back to me all excited. "Allie's driving out here for your show tonight."

"Another country girl who disapproves?" I ask. It gives me great pleasure to give her a hard time about not liking my music.

"Actually, she's the black sheep of the family and loves it."

"Hmm." I grin. "Maybe I picked the wrong sister." I don't mean a word of it, but Abby slams a fist into my chest and laughs.

"Don't be a jerk," she says as I pull her into a hug. "Besides, she's a divorced single mom. I'm not sure you could handle the daddy thing."

"You're right about that."

We start walking away from the alley, not like there was going to be any action there anyway. Abby doesn't seem to be the public sex type...at least, not yet.

"So what sort of baggage are you carrying?" I ask. *What are you hiding, Ms. Reporter?*

"I'm too boring for baggage. It's just me, my studio apartment, and my dog. You do like dogs, right?"

So she's still not interested in admitting the *ScandalLust* deal? Fine. Maybe there's really nothing to it.

"I guess if we're a couple now, it doesn't matter whether or not I like dogs."

We turn back onto the main road and I'm relieved to not see any paps. They've got to be somewhere though. They don't just leave.

"Couple? Are you referring to us as a couple?" Abby's voice is a mix of curiosity and hesitation.

"It wasn't me. It was Kirsty back there at the shoot. And if a photo shoot director who works for some magazine says we're a couple, then..."

"Then we're a couple," she finishes. "I mean, that's the going standard for determining a relationship, right?"

I laugh at her, grateful she can be lighthearted and understand my sarcasm. I'm still not sure about this whole relationship thing, but if I'm going to attempt to spend time with only one woman, I'm glad it's Abby.

"I've got an idea," I tell her. "You like adventures?"

She looks at me, a little confused. "I think so."

On the way over here, I saw an indoor shooting range. It's one place I doubt the paps would try to sneak in, and seeing my girl in her leather pants and corset wielding a firearm is too sexy to pass up.

I lead the way, and when we walk in, she smiles. "I can handle this type of adventure."

"Oh, can you?"

She's awfully sure of herself.

I check behind us to confirm there's no one following with a camera, and then we check-in at the sales counter. After filling out forms and paying for ammo, the guy at the counter leads us to the back and arms us with a Glock 22.

"Want to go for the cartoon deer?" I ask, pointing to the choices for paper targets.

"No animals." She goes soft on me and grabs a generic circle target.

I clip the target into place and push the switch to move it into position.

"Want me to go first to show you?" I offer. I take the gun magazine and start loading it with the ammo I bought.

At first, I'm second-guessing whether this was a good idea. She seems timid. Maybe she's afraid of guns and I should've picked something less intense for us to do. But then she shakes her head and laughs.

"Move out of my way," she demands.

I'm caught off guard and let her take over, watching to see what she does. She grabs the magazine and inserts the rest of the bullets with ease. Then loads the gun, and sets it down. She puts on her eye and ear protection, handing me my own to do the same. Then I watch her pick the gun back up, adjust her grip, steady her aim, and fire.

Before I get a chance to react to her perfect shot, hitting the bullseye right in the center, she fires again. Another great shot. I stand there speechless as she empties the magazine, not one bullet missing the target. When she finishes, she sets the gun down, and turns to me, waiting for my reaction.

"I have no words." My surprise amuses her.

She pulls off her earplugs and goggles. "You okay?"

"Where the hell did you learn to shoot like that?"

She laughs. "My dad. He had me and Allie aiming at empty cans in the backyard as soon as we were old enough to take a steady shot."

"Wow. Must be a hell of a guy."

"Yeah," she says, but her face drops. She looks distant. "He was."

Was. "Is he?"

"He died when I was thirteen. We didn't do much target practice after that..."

"What happened?" Curiosity gets the best of me, but I have no business asking. "Never mind. That's your personal life. I shouldn't have—"

"He killed himself," she says quietly. "He always was full of surprises. All those guns he collected, and he went out by overdosing on my mom's prescription pills."

"That's awful."

"It was."

"You guys sound like you were close too."

She nods and I can see her heart breaking just thinking about it. "We were. It was a long time ago, though. We got through it, somehow. And we learned not to take any part of life for granted, so..." She shrugs. "I refuse to minimize who he was down to his last moments. I had thirteen unforgettable years with him before he made the worst decision of his life. I hold on to those thirteen years."

Not sure how to respond, I put my safety gear on the counter and wrap my arms around her. She clings to me, and the warmth of our bodies together makes us both relax. My sweet, small town girl just got a million times more complicated, and her willingness to confide in me makes me like her that much more.

Told you she was trouble.

Chapter Five

Abby

Miles retrieves my target and suggests we get back to the bus before it leaves us behind on its trek to tonight's hotel. I'm tempted to call him out for not shooting, but I don't want to lose that moment we just had. I don't mind talking about my dad. He was an important part of my life, and losing him changed who I was. I like that Miles asked. Most people run from the slightest mention of an uncomfortable topic. But he could handle it. It makes me like him that much more, which terrifies me at the same time. What's going on between us?

I watch as Miles folds up my target into a smaller square. "And what are your plans with that?" I ask.

"I'm keeping it as a souvenir...and a reminder not to mess with you."

It feels good to laugh. The air around us lightens, and I'm left wondering how two people, who are so different, can be naturally great together.

We head back toward the bus, but quickly find out where the paps went when they couldn't stay on our tail. They're hanging around the tour bus, and the only way to get onto it will be through them.

"Shit," Miles says when he sees them.

"Should we make a run for it?"

"Nah." His body goes tense. "I'll deal with them." One of his hands still grips mine, but I look down and see his other clenched into a fist.

We keep our stride and walk up to them with an air of authority. As soon as one of them spots us, the others swing around, all cameras pointed our way.

"You all need to get the hell out of here be- fore I make you leave," Miles tells them.

I look up at the tinted bus windows but don't see any movement inside. The rest of the band must not be back yet. It's just us and the ratz.

One of them moves a camera away from his face and steps closer. "Who's your girlfriend, Miles? Can you tell us where you were? What are your plans today before the show? Can you tell us anything about your sister and her recent scandal?"

I don't know what he's talking about with Kennedy, but the barrage of questions is suf- focating.

"Fuck you guys. Stay away from Kennedy. Stay away from us." He gets in the pap's face, close enough to make the guy lose his balance and stumble back.

They're holding their position though, not going away, not letting us get onto the bus. Miles shoves the guy and starts toward the one closest to the door. I see his arm tense and rise, like he's going to punch the guy, but he looks past the pap, past the bus, and something catches his eye that makes him even angrier.

I have to stand on my tiptoes to see what the rest of them are seeing. A black car just pulled up, and the back door stands open with none other than Devon Stone stepping out. Yeah, this just got far worse. I squeeze past the pap ratz and reach Miles, grabbing his arm. It's hard as a rock from the tension, but I pull on him to break his focus.

"Come on. We don't need to deal with this."

He doesn't say anything, just shakes his arm loose and marches toward Devon. Great. We've got cameras aimed and ready to capture the brawl that's inevitably about to break out in the middle of the street. I nervously glance around, praying the rest of the band shows up soon. Nate and Dax can control Miles, pull him away and get him to listen. Kennedy can deal with her own boyfriend.

"I thought you were supposed to be half-way around the world," Miles says, angrily.

That's when I remember the stuff I found in the bus. The condom wrapper and lingerie. Maybe he found out she's cheating on him. Or maybe I'm being overly paranoid.

"Plans changed. Where's Kennedy?" Devon asks. His face is serious, like Miles is the last person he wanted to run into.

"At a shoot at Studio 99. What are you doing out here?"

By now, we're in arm's reach of each other next to Devon's ride. I'm not about to jump in between them again. My heart pounds and my hands are damp with sweat at the thought of these two getting into an argument. They could kill each other if they wanted to.

"What's it matter to you?" Devon asks, getting defensive.

The camera guys inch closer, snapping a hundred shots a minute. I take a deep breath and let out a sigh. This isn't going to end well. But then Miles looks down at me. Our eyes meet and I plead with him through unspoken words to let things go.

He looks back at Devon. "Look man. I'm not in the mood for more of this shit between us. Whatever goes on between you and Kennedy, that's your business. But these guys," he points to the ratz, "they want to make it their business too. I'm going to protect her." I assume he means Kennedy, but my heart flutters all the same.

"Then it sounds like we have the same intention." Devon drops his shoulders a little. "I don't need big brother getting in my way though. Let Kennedy run Kennedy's life, and you and I won't have any more problems."

Miles spreads his arms wide. "Hey man. I can admit I've acted like an asshole to you.

But the future may be very different, so why don't we just leave the past behind and call a truce?"

Devon hesitates. Maybe this higher road thing will backfire, making Miles look like a pushover.

"Fair enough." Then Devon extends his hand and Miles shakes it. More shutter clicks from the cameras. "You know we have plans for you guys." He taps on the glass of the car and the driver's side door opens. "It works in all our favors to stay on each other's good sides."

The guy who gets out of the car is enormous. Taller than both the guys, and big enough to be a bodybuilder. He's dressed in a black suit, and without direction, he walks toward the paparazzi guys and casually rests his hand on the belt holster carrying a gun. Devon showed up with his own security. Nice.

The paps scatter the second the guy says the word, "Move." Once they scurry to their car and drive away, the guy returns to the car, leaving me speechless and Miles and Devon laughing.

"I should get me one of those. Saves my fists a lot of trouble," Miles says.

Devon leaves to find Kennedy, and Miles and I get onto the bus.

"That was...intense," I say.

Miles hardly seems fazed, just a little on edge. Seeing me a little shaken up, he laughs, catching me more off guard.

"You can shoot a target with ease and accuracy, but a couple guys talking and some jackasses taking photos is intense?"

Should I even bring up the part where Devon and Miles just got into a big fight days ago?

"Okay, fine, tough guy. Maybe I'm just a timid, simple girl who's still dealing with the culture shock of being involved with you."

We're near the couches now, and Miles sits down, watching me with amusement. As I pass him to take a seat next to him, he grabs me by my waist and pulls me onto him as he lies back on the cushions. I let out a yelp of surprise, but his hands run down my back and grip my ass, and I'm overcome with the lust I felt earlier during the photo shoot.

"Hey," I say, inches away from his face.

His gaze is dark, and I feel his hand reach up to the back of my head. "Did I mention how ungodly sexy you look right now?"

My cheeks go warm as he pulls me to his mouth, kissing me hard. The corset top feels like it's strangling me as I try to find my breath. I entangle my fingers into his hair and savor the taste of him, but I want more. I pull away from his mouth, kissing his lips, his chin, his neck. I fumble at the buttons of his shirt, tugging it away from his firm, tattooed chest. My lips make a trail of kisses where my tongue wants to draw a complete map. But I want more. I move down to his stomach, to the sexy lines where his abs collide with his hips. I unbutton his jeans and slowly pull down the zipper, and he finally figures out where I want this to go.

I massage at his hardness constrained inside his pants and want to set him free, but as soon as my nails graze the waistline of his boxer briefs, an eruption of noise plummets onto the bus. Footsteps and hollering.

"Whoa! What are we walking in on?" Nate asks excitedly. He and Dax plop down in the chairs in front of us as though they're going to be our audience.

I awkwardly stand up, mortified, while Miles just lies there with his shirt undone and pants unzipped. If I could take a mental snapshot to hold on to forever, this would be it. He looks gorgeous, and my body screams with lust. I want to yell at these buffoons to get the hell off the bus and let me finish what I started, but then the driver appears and sits down behind the wheel. Eddie pulls up behind us in his car and honks. And I see Devon and Kennedy get into the black car with the huge security guard driving.

Guess our time is up. Miles sits up and I drop down next to him, tense and desperately in need of some alone time with my rock star. The sexual spark between us has grown into a raging fire today, and I know he's feeling it too. I need him to claim me. To take me the way he did yesterday at the hotel. I want his hands and mouth possessing me, and I don't want any more interruptions.

Tonight. After the show. And nothing's going to stop us.

*

"I'm so happy you made it!" I throw my arms around Allie the second she gets out of her car outside of tonight's venue.

"You kidding? I haven't seen you in forever. Plus, I'll take a night off where I can get one." She pulls away and surveys me. "And what have *you* been up to? The spunky hair, that outfit. Where'd my angel of a big sister go?"

"Oh stop." I drag her in through the backstage entrance. The noise from inside tells me

Tempest's set is starting. Damn. I was going to introduce Allie to Miles. She has no idea he and I are together. And when she finds out, she's going to flip.

We take our places, just off of stage left, and I do my best not to gawk at Miles like a fan girl. I'm just having a hard time believing everything that's happening. I can't help myself and grab my phone from my pocket, taking a short video of him starting on the first song. He's wearing a tight white shirt, and like x-ray vision I can imagine every dip and crevice of his abs. He's in torn jeans, and his hair is still somewhat styled from this morning's photo shoot. Then again, it's also a little disheveled from my inability to keep my hands off him. The look works for him, and he looks sexier than ever.

"Have I told you lately how incredibly jealous I am of your life," Allie yells over the music.

I look and smile at her. "It's not a bad gig." I remember how I felt days ago, when it was the worst assignment of my life. Funny how much things can change when you have Miles to sway your opinion.

I find myself dancing to the music, hearing it in an entirely different way. I've never been a fan of loud, raging rock or incoherent lyrics, but knowing these people, their lives, the songs take on a new meaning. Allie's loving it too, but she's always been into this scene. I used to think she was the weird one, but it's clear I've been too quick to judge all these years.

The first song ends, transitioning seamlessly into the second. It's even louder, and the crowd goes nuts. A mosh pit forms, and I laugh out loud at my memory of my first and last experience in the middle of one of those. That was less than a week ago. How have things changed so much?

Miles looks over at us and gives a nod and smile. Our eyes meet, and that sexy gaze of his is full of so many promises. Allie fails to

notice that, and instead assumes he was looking at her.

"I think guitar guy's got a thing for me.
You think I have a chance?" Her voice is
dreamy as she shouts over the music.

"Um... He's taken," I tell her.

"Oh please. He's a rock star. He'll gladly be
taken every night by a different girl, I'm
sure."

I think back to how Miles was before. But
he's different now. He doesn't want that anymore. I'm sure of it.

Allie continues, "You said there's an after
party later?"

"Yeah."

"You've got between now and then to tell
me everything you know about this guy. I'm
going for it."

My face warms with what I'm about to admit right in front of Miles. "I assure you. I
know he's seeing someone, and he's a one-
woman guy." I hope.

"And what makes you so sure?"

She turns to me, and I don't have to answer. The confession has to be all over my face.

"You're a liar," she says.

I laugh and shake my head no. "I don't know how it happened, but yeah...he and I are—"

"Fucking? Are you fucking him?"

"Seeing each other," I correct her. It's much more than sex.

Allie looks from me to Miles and back at me. "And now I'm that much more jealous. How could you not tell me?"

"I was going to introduce you to him. I wanted you to meet him and see he's not just some sex god rock star."

"But is he?" she asks, her eyes beaming with excitement. "A sex god rock star?"

My face must be bright red at this point. "That's beside the point."

She squeals with delight. "Okay, you get that one. What about the other guys?"

I look at Nate and Dax. "Go for it. You can probably get both at once."

"Ooh." She considers this for a second. "Goals."

Chapter Six

Abby

The set finishes, and Miles walks offstage directly toward me. He doesn't bother stopping, and presses into me, kissing me with his guitar still strapped around him.

"You like the show?"

"I did." I kiss him again. "And I liked you."

"Glad to see you're coming around."

I hear someone clear their throat behind me.

"Oh. This is my sister. Allie, Miles. Miles, Allie. She drove out for the show."

He shakes her hand, and I notice Dax checking her out from behind. Miles nods for him to join us, and Dax walks over, joining our little group. The guys are coated in sweat, and standing close to Miles, I can feel his heart racing. It's sexy.

"Dax, Allie," I say. "Allie, Dax."

Dax puts his arm around Allie like they're old friends. "You're both coming to the party right?"

"Absolutely," Allie says, her eyes glued to Dax. I suppose between Nate and Dax, this is the guy I'd seduce. Nate is just too much of a...I don't know...a manwhore.

Miles looks at me and raises an eyebrow. Yeah, I'm pretty sure my sister's going to be Dax's groupie of the night. Whatever, as long as she's okay with one-night stands.

"It's back at the hotel. You want to head over now?" Miles asks. "The roadies can finish up here."

"Actually, I'll ride with Allie and meet you there." I step up on my tiptoes to kiss him again. "We have a long night ahead of us," I promise him.

Miles wraps his arms around my hips and pulls me closer. His tongue dances with mine, and when he pulls away, I'm breathless. I don't think anyone ever kissed me the way Miles does.

Without a word, he slaps Dax on the back and they walk off. Allie's lingering gaze tells me she's perfectly content moving on from Miles to Dax. I think she's always wanted to date a rock star, and it has more to do with the title than the person.

"Wow," is all she says. "Need another reporter on your assignment?"

"You're a preschool teacher."

We find her car, and I direct her toward the hotel. Apparently, the rooftop's been blocked off for us, courtesy of the Stones, and the guest list is limited to Stone VIPs and friends of the band—meaning me, Allie, and whoever Nate finds between the venue and here.

When we pull up, valet is ready and waiting. Inside, the line extends to the door, with most people being turned away.

"Exclusive crowd, huh?" Allie asks.

"Yeah. I bet the label's trying to schmooze the band even more. Probably means there'll be great food and drinks upstairs."

Someone with a clipboard spots us at the end of the line. They call out, "Abigail Clarke, right?"

I nod. Have I just been recognized?

He waves us over and escorts us to the front of the line. We skip the waiting process and are brought right to the elevator where he uses an access key to get us up to the penthouse.

"Enjoy your evening, ladies," he tells us when the doors open up again.

We step off the elevator and walk down the short hall to a set of closed double doors and a security guard waiting out front. This one I recognize. He's Devon's driver, the big guy who scared off the paps earlier.

"Evening, Ms. Clarke." He nods and opens a door for us.

"Thank you."

Allie is staring wide-eyed. "When did you become VIP famous? When you started sleeping with the guitarist?"

"Not likely. These people are just being nice."

"Forget nice. They know you. You've got to hook me up with your contacts. I want exclusive access."

"Don't you have plans of hooking up with your own contact?"

She shoves me playfully with her elbow. "So how serious are you two?"

"Me and Dax? Well..." I laugh at her as she rolls her eyes. We approach the bar and get a couple cocktails. This open bar might lead to trouble. After our drinks are ready we take them to a quiet corner. The penthouse has been all done up with plush couches, high top tables, elaborate lights overhead, and a deejay on the far side of the room. Glass doors open beyond to a balcony where I think I glimpse a pool. It's sort of funny to me. The place looks pretty glamorous but everyone's dressed casually. I prefer it much more to the elaborate formal events.

Miles and the band should be here anytime. I keep glancing toward the front doors as I talk to Allie.

"Spill it, girl," she tells me.

"He wrote me a song. What's that say about how *serious* we are?" I really am asking. I mean, who does that as a means to get a girl's attention?

"A Tempest song? Did they play it tonight?"

"No. This one was just for me. You know, my style. He even got an acoustic guitar and..." I drift away remembering that night. It was the greatest surprise I've ever received.

"So he's got a sweet side. Damn. I'm even more jealous now."

"There's something about him. He's...mysterious, yet what you see is what you get."

"And I take it you've gotten a whole lot of what you've seen?"

We both burst out laughing. "I'm not talking to you about him like that."

"Oh please, if you're going to date a rock star, you can't be a prude." She sips from her drink. I'm tempted to chug mine. "Is he as good in bed as he is at guitar?"

"Better," I blurt out. "But seriously, I think I really like him."

She smiles, knowing I haven't been much of a relationship person in a long while. "And how does he feel about you?"

I think about that loaded question. I can only base it off our short amount of time together, but... "I think he feels the same."

Arms wrap around me from behind, and I almost jump. But Miles has grown familiar to me in that same way a favorite t-shirt evokes an entirely different mood in you. His touch and smell...and taste...all bring me immense comfort. I spin around and find myself face to face with him.

"Took you long enough," I say, my lips curving into a grin.

He nibbles at my neck before coming around and sitting next to me. "Had to get a few things squared away."

My curiosity perks up. Maybe we should've stayed long enough to see what more the band was up to. But that's just the reporter in me butting in. It's none of my business. They probably just needed to help load things onto the trailer.

"Where are the others?"

Before Miles answers, Dax shows up with his hands full of overflowing shot glasses. He places one in front of each of us. Nate follows behind with two girls attached to his sides. We make room for everyone to sit. I spot Kennedy on the other side of the room, but Devon's with her, and judging by her roaming hands on his body, it's obvious she's busy.

"To a great show and a great night," Dax says, holding his shot glass.

The rest of us follow suit and lift our glasses. "Cheers!" I forget to ask what's in it, before taking the shot in one gulp. The overpowering taste of cinnamon burns, filling my chest with warmth.

The glasses clatter back down on the table, and Dax stands back up, taking my sister's hand this time. Without asking, he pulls her out toward the makeshift dance floor near the deejay. Just before they're out of sight, I hear him proclaim loudly, "Let's get this party started!"

*

The strangest part of hanging out with rock stars is realizing how many rock star friends they have. And not just those in the rock scene. It feels like Stone Records brought in every major name signed to them for tonight's party. Are they trying to make a point?

"Can I ask you something?" I turn to Miles, who's just downed another shot.

He cocks an eyebrow waiting for me to continue.

"What's the point in all this? You've got Stone Records trying to seduce you, but if they want you, why don't you just sign with them?"

A smile stretches across his face and he drops a hand down to my thigh. The warmth of his touch spreads all over. "We've got Stone in one corner. Rev Records in the other corner. It's a boxing match, and we're the spectators right now. We're letting them battle it out a little longer because the contract we end up signing will be that much juicier. It's good to have options." His eyes scan the room full of important bodies all here to celebrate with Tempest. "It'll only get better from here."

He waves over a server and gets us a couple more drinks, this time a cocktail for me. I'm halfway through it when he leans in, his eyes intense. "By the way, I think we need to talk."

My heart skips a beat. Those words have never meant anything good. Is something wrong? Is he realizing, as we sit here at this party, that he doesn't want to be tied down to only me?

"Sure," I say. "Now?"

He doesn't answer but nudges me to get up. I follow behind as he leads us outside. Last time we were on a balcony, Devon Stone tried to kill him. I automatically find myself looking around, checking over our shoulders.

It's busy out here but not as bad as inside. It's a huge balcony with lounge areas sectioned off to allow some privacy. Miles brings us to an empty corner—dark, with a small love seat facing away from everyone else. My heart pounds as I think of all the worst-case scenarios that could happen right now.

He could dump me. He could confess something awful. He could tell me I disgust him and everything we've done has been a terrible mistake.

"Sit." He waits for me to settle and then drops down next to me.

I try to keep my hands steady and not give away my concern. Just as he's about to speak, his phone rings. He pulls it from his pocket and declines the call. A notification pops up saying he's had three missed phone calls. It makes me even more suspicious, but at this point, I'm praying I'm just acting paranoid.

"Everything okay?" I ask.

"No," he says bluntly.

Dammit. I knew something bad was about to happen.

He stands up and goes to the ledge of the balcony a couple feet in front of me. He leans against it, and I can't help but watch his arms flex as he does. Then he spins around, looking at me, his eyes blazing.

"All day, you've been looking like that." He takes a step closer. "And all day, we've been getting interrupted." Another step, and I have to look up to see him. Though it's almost too dark to see anything at all, I can make out enough of his facial features to see the lust filling his eyes. My heart skips a beat. "I need you. And nothing's stopping us this time."

He drops to his knees, grabs me by the back of my head, and pulls me into an intense kiss. His tongue plunges past my lips, massaging my own. His breath is shaky and he tastes like liquor. My legs wrap around his waist and pull him in closer to me. I press my hands against his firm chest, gripping and clawing at his tight shirt. Miles's mouth moves down my neck and over my breasts spilling out over the lacy white corset. Every time his tongue touches my skin, a shock of heat rushes through me. I feel myself aching for him.

But...

I break away and look around.

"We can't here. It's too..." Public?

"I assure you, no one knows we're even over here. They all want to be a part of the party, not on the sidelines."

God, it's tempting. The alcohol coursing through me is making me feel bolder by the second, but if we did something out here, right here, right now, it would be so out of character for me.

Wait. Everything that's been happening between me and Miles has been out of character for me, and I like it.

I kiss him, sucking on his bottom lip as I pull away. "I'm not exactly accessible with these leather pants."

He laughs. "Please. We just have to improvise."

His hands trail down the front of my body, grazing my breasts, my stomach. He reaches the apex of my thighs and pulls my legs apart. With his thumbs, he starts massaging my aching folds through my clothes, adding just enough pressure to make me want more.

"We have to be," I try to speak through uneven breaths, "discreet." Drawing attention would inevitably lead to photos finding their way online. It would be mortifying.

"I bet I can fuck you with all our clothes on."

That doesn't even make sense. I smile, trying to be more flirty than undeniably horny. "Prove it."

He lets out a groan as he stands up. He sits down next to me, grabbing me in the process, and pulling me on top of him. Straddling him, I can feel just how hard he is. And for a moment, I thought he was sick of me.

A giggle escapes me as we make out like a couple of juveniles. Our hands groping, our mouths claiming as much of each other as we can reach. I want him in me, and at this point I don't care who sees. I fumble with the button on his jeans, awkwardly undoing it. I reach for the zipper, pulling it down, and then I scoot back so I can move his jeans and boxers out of the way, freeing him. At the same time, he unfastens my pants and reaches around, cupping my ass in his hands. He slides me up against his growing cock, and I wrap my hands, one on top of the other, around him, holding firm as I push him against my throbbing cleft. I still have no idea how he thinks he'll be able to enter me in this position, and he better figure it out quick. After a day of teasing, my body is overflowing with tension and ready to be unraveled.

"Stand up," he quietly demands.

I don't want to put more space between us, but I obey. Stepping away from him, I feel like we're opposite ends of a magnet. We can't be kept apart.

Miles spins me around so that I'm facing the balcony. That's unfair. Now I can't feel him or see him.

I wait.

I hear him fumbling with something. Then his phone rings again. There's the sound of the click as he declines another call. Then the sound of foil ripping. My man came prepared.

In a swift motion, he grips the waistline of my pants, yanking them down to mid-thigh. The sudden exposure of my ass fills me with self-awareness. If anyone walked over here right now...

He pulls me back onto his lap, his erection pressed between us. My pants are constricting against my thighs, making it hard for me to move at all. I feel bound, like he's tied me up, and just that thought makes me wetter. Miles grips my thighs with his strong fingers, exploring the little bit of skin exposed. He traces along the elastic of my thong, teasing the hot skin underneath.

"Ready?" he asks. I'm not sure if his choice of word is meant to be a consideration to my feelings or a sexy warning.

"I've wanted this all day."

That's all the permission he needs. He lifts me up, slides my thong to the side, and pulls me down on top of him, burying his cock deep inside of me.

It takes everything in my power not to scream. With my own lack of mobility, I'm at his mercy. He sets the rhythm, lifting my hips and dropping me down. The slick feel of him sliding in and out sends relief through me. God, I needed him too. With my legs bound at the thighs by my pants, my own body squeezes him with each motion. I feel every inch of him.

I arch my back to feel more of his body behind me. I turn toward his ear and let out a moan only he can hear. His hips buck even harder at the sound, so I do it again. I want him harder, faster, and he gets the hint.

My breath comes out in gasps as Miles takes me. With each inhale from him, I feel his body shudder. His teeth graze my back as he seeks something to stifle his own growls of satisfaction.

I can't take any more. At the hands of Miles, my body is quickly coming undone. Warmth courses through my veins and into my core. I feel myself clenching tighter to him, and tiny ripples of ecstasy set me off on a point of no return.

"Come for me," Miles demands.

As the first scream escapes me, he quickly covers my mouth with his hand. His hips do the work as I bite into his palm. My entire body seems to explode into fragments as an orgasm rips through me. My own release brings him to his peak, and he slams his head into my back, gripping me tighter to him, as he comes. Our bodies still as one, we take a minute to recover, gasping for breath. I turn my face toward his again, kissing him. His mouth is fiery hot, yet his tongue is gentle this time. His lips linger on mine before we break away.

"Told you," is all he says, with a grin.

For a moment, the entire party had disappeared. It was just me and Miles. Now, I'm overwhelmingly aware of what we just did in front of all these people. I lift myself off of Miles, quickly readjusting my panties and pulling my pants back up. I look around cautiously.

"Relax. Like I said," Miles lifts his hips and fixes his own clothes, "they're all too busy in their own worlds to notice."

He seems to be right. Not a single person appears to be looking this way.

That is, until I notice someone several feet away, leaning against the wall. My heart stops, and I let out a gasp.

Miles stands up and swivels around. "Eddie? The fuck?"

"If you two are done, we need to talk."

Chapter Seven

Abby

Eddie tells him to meet him at the downstairs bar in five. Miles kisses me and leaves to find a bathroom. I stay behind, trying to recover from shock. I should be utterly mortified right now, but I'm having a hard time caring. Instead, adrenaline leaves me laughing like a lunatic. I can't believe we just did that.

I brush my fingers through my hair and give myself a once over. Hoping I don't look like I just had sex, I head back inside to find Allie. I find her at the bar, flirting with the bartender and finishing a drink just as he sets another in front of her.

"Hey. Where'd your dance partner go?" I ask. I don't want her getting carried away with the drinks tonight, but I also want to make sure she has a good time.

"Eh. He's around." Her voice is a little hesitant. I hope nothing bad happened. "Last I saw, he was talking to the girl who won Artist of the Year at the HIT Awards last year."

"Well, I don't want you drinking alone." I take a seat next to her and order a white wine for myself.

"Oh, she's not alone," a voice says from behind me. I turn and see Kennedy coming over. She sits on the empty stool on the other side of Allie. "We were having some girl time." She gives me her fake smile, and I'm filled with dread. Great. The last person I want my sister hanging out with.

"Where's Devon?" I ask Kennedy. Shouldn't she be too distracted by him to bother us?

"Ugh." Kennedy downs another shot of something. "He had to leave early. A conference call or something. Trust me, girls. Date an ordinary guy. Getting involved with powerful men is just asking for trouble." She's got her eyes glued to me the whole time. Great, so she's still throwing her vague threats at me. "Speaking of, where's my brother?"

"He had something to do." I turn away from her, focusing on my glass instead.

Kennedy lets out a cackle. "Something to *do*. Probable a six-foot tall brunette, if you know what I mean."

Allie looks from Kennedy to me, not sure what to think of this. Her hand goes to her head, and I notice there's a bigger problem.

"You okay?" I ask.

"Yeah," she says, slowly. "I'm fine. Let's dance." She hops off the stool, her balance wavering for a second, and then pulls me along with her to the dance floor. I should've been in here earlier, keeping an eye on how much she was drinking. It's obvious she's far more drunk than I am right now.

"So where have you been?" she asks, turning to face me.

I'm not much of a dancer, but the quick-paced industrial music playing leaves everyone jumping around. No talent necessary. "With Miles," I answer Allie.

"You sure he's a good guy?"

Woah. That question came out of nowhere. "Yeah. Why?"

"I've been talking to your friend, Kennedy. She doesn't seem to agree."

Of course. "Kennedy's just bored. Ignore her."

"I don't know, Ab. I mean, she *is* his sister. She knows him better than...better than you do."

It's hard to have a serious conversation with Allie, when half her words are slurred, but Kennedy had no right to make Miles look bad in front of Allie. "She's lying."

"She said he had a threesome last week. And that he's with a different woman every night."

"Well, he's not like that anymore. He's different with me."

"Oh, Abby." She puts a hand on my shoulder. "You've seen too many movies. Guys don't change." She spins around, checking out the people around her. "You've got lots of options. You're beautiful. You're smart. You deserve a guy who—who loves you for you and doesn't make you change for him."

What is she saying? "I haven't changed for him."

She touches my hair. "No?"

I swat her hand away. "No. The hair was Kennedy's idea. The clothes are from a photo shoot." What do I need to say to get it through to her? Miles is not a bad guy. So what if he had a bad reputation before? He just hadn't met the right person. He hadn't met me.

"I'm sorry," she says over the music. "I don't want you to get hurt. And he's the type of guy that hurts people."

I shake my head to object. Allie stops dancing and looks at me with a dead serious expression. "You know what I've been through. You just have to trust me..." She drifts off like she's daydreaming. "And you know what else?"

"What?"

"I...I—" She covers her mouth with her hand. "I think I'm going to be sick."

I go into crisis mode and lead Allie to the closest bathroom. She barely makes it before hurling in the toilet. My stomach turns.

"Don't be mad at me," she pleads.

"Don't believe everything you hear from strangers," I spit back. I am mad. Pissed at her for not giving Miles the benefit of the doubt. And livid at Kennedy for opening her big mouth.

"Was she lying? About the threesome? About the one-night stands?"

I can't answer. It's technically true, but...I have to believe people can change. Miles seems to really care about me. I hated his music last week. That changed. So couldn't his bad habits have changed as well?

"Your silence is very revealing," she says. Allie washes up and dries her hands, still unstable on her feet.

"Let's get you back to the hotel room. You can sleep it off."

"Right. Listen," she says. "I'm sorry. I know you like him. But Kennedy said—"

"You really don't get it. Kennedy has been battling against me since day one. She's manipulative and conniving. She doesn't think I'm good for Miles, and she's trying to drive me away. She wasn't being nice to you, Allie. She was using you."

Allie considers this for a second before stumbling out of the bathroom. I follow behind, but she's moving fast, on a mission. She goes back to the bar where Kennedy is now the one flirting with the bartender. Not slowing down, and not giving any warning, Allie reaches out and shoves Kennedy. Pushed off the stool, she nearly plummets to the ground but catches herself at the last moment.

"What the hell, bitch?" She turns to Allie right as I catch up.

I step in between the two of them.

"What's your problem?" Kennedy asks me, her eyes burning with new rage. "You siccing your sister after me now? Can't do your own dirty work?"

I don't even think. One second I'm trying to do damage control, the next, my hand is flying into Kennedy's face. I smack her hard. "Leave Allie alone. And leave *me* alone."

I turn my back on her. "Let's go," I tell Allie.

We storm toward the door to leave. I don't know how I'm going to explain this to Miles, and I wish he'd been here to prevent all of it.

"Hey Abby!" Kennedy's behind us, yelling now. I swing around ready for a full-blown fight. "This isn't over. I know what your real motives are, and I swear I'll bring you down. Watch your back."

* * *

Miles

Leave it to Eddie to try and ruin my night. If I knew he was going to constantly act like my parent on this tour, I would've convinced him to stay in L.A.

What the hell were you thinking going to a shooting range with a reporter? Do you have any idea how that can backfire?

So sorry, pops. Maybe I'm a master of *not* thinking.

I push through the doors back into the party. He killed the high I was feeling after fucking Abby. Now I'm just pissed. Maybe I'll track her down for another quickie to cheer up.

"Hey, brother!" Someone slaps me on the back, and I spin around ready to shove him out of my way.

"Landers." It's my buddy from Cylon Smash. "What the hell brings you out here?"

"The whole band's been chilling in Texas. Then we find out the big guys of Tempest are here and having a party. I just wanted to stop in and check out what fame looks like."

"Looks a lot like extravagance and over-protection from your handlers." I start toward the bar, knowing he'll follow. Abby's probably back at the table with her sister, so I grab a whisky double and head that way.

"What's that mean? Handlers?"

I shake my head. "It's nothing. Management being management, and I'm not a fan of being managed, if you know what I mean."

We get back to the table and find it nearly empty. Kennedy is sitting there twirling a straw in her tall drink. Landers plops down next to her. He's always had a thing for my sister, even hooked up with her once.

"You're looking lonesome tonight," he says, moving in close.

"Where'd Devon run off to?" I ask, and at the mention of his name, Landers moves away from her and checks over his shoulder.

"Back to the hotel. Had work stuff to do." She looks up at me, glaring. "And your girl-friend left with her sister. One of them can't handle their alcohol."

Damn. So much for a quickie to bring back my good mood.

Kennedy turns to Landers. "I don't suppose you brought anything that can help liven things up?" Her hand disappears under the table, touching god knows what, to convince him. She winks at him, and his whole face lights up. I don't get it. What's the big deal with Ken?

"As a matter of fact..." He looks from her to me. "You sure as hell need a smoke. Come on."

The three of us make our way back out onto the balcony. I glance over to the love seat
that was occupied by me and Abby just moments ago. A crowd of people have found
their way to the private area, destroying its
appeal. We end up at the edge of the balcony
looking over the busy street below.

Landers leans against the ledge while Ken
and I take a seat at a high top table. Landers
reaches into his pocket and finds a joint,
lighting it and passing it to Kennedy. "Ladies
first."

I take a gulp of my drink to drown out Eddie's lectures. He could've had the decency to
wait until tomorrow rather than bothering
me about my screw ups tonight. Kennedy
hands the joint to me and I take a couple
puffs, my head finally clearing.

We smoke the whole thing while Landers
tells us all about Cylon's recent successes.
They're getting better gigs, Ender, the lead
singer, is causing trouble with his hook-ups,
and they've yet to find a manager who can

"respect their view", as he puts it. I don't know. He drags on and on about it as the high takes over all of us. After awhile, the only news he can think to share is how their drummer likes sticking French fries in his milkshakes. Just that mention makes us all hungry, and Landers leaves to find us drinks—clearly confusing liquor with sustenance.

He waltzes away, and Kennedy laughs, a big smile on her face. Her eyes are glazed over, but she seems relaxed.

"So Eddie was looking for you," she says.

Thanks for bringing that back up. "Yeah, I talked to him."

"What was that about?" she asks, her words coming out slowly.

I finish my drink and look around for someone who'll get me another faster than Landers. "He needed to chew me out for going to a gun range with Abby today."

"That was dumb, don't you think?"

Kennedy's the only one who knows everything about my past. Of course she'd take Eddie's side on this. "No one saw us go in. It was just me and Abby there."

"Right. But if someone *did* see you. If they *did... see you...*" She starts giggling like those are the funniest words ever. "You know what would happen. You really want to throw everything away for some random woman you're screwing?"

It's hard to really see her as being thoughtful when she's high as a kite. One of the caterers walks by with a tray of sliders. We take the whole thing and tell them to go get us some shots.

Digging into the food, I say, "She's not just some random woman. I like her. You need to give her a chance."

Kennedy rolls her eyes. "Right. The last time I gave one of your girlfriends a chance, she used us both."

She's right. My last serious girlfriend ended up in bed with Devon Stone. That's the

last time I attempted a relationship with anyone, but I don't get that vibe from Abby.
"Abby wouldn't do that. She's not like..." I
drift off and take another bite of my food instead. Shots of bourbon appear at our table,
and I'm grateful. I throw back one before
Kennedy pushes another toward me. She lifts
hers up like she's giving a toast.

"I'll give her a chance if you stop risking
everything you've worked hard to change for
yourself." She clinks the glass against mine,
not waiting for my response.

She doesn't understand Abby's worth the
risk, but it's not going to get bad again. Hell,
smoking pot in public was just as dangerous
for me, but neither her nor Eddie are out here
ripping me a new asshole for that. These people need to pick their priorities. Whatever. I
drink the shot anyway.

"You know," I say, mostly thinking out
loud. "It's all fucking Eddie's fault anyway.
He's got to make up his mind. Either he wants
me to seduce the reporter, or he wants me to

steer clear of her." I let out a laugh. It all sounds so absurd to me.

"What are you talking about?" Her interest is piqued and I'm lacking a filter to care what I say.

"Fucking Eddie. He says she's on tour with us to make us look good. He says we have to make her fall for one of us to make sure we stay on her good side. He says it's all part of a ploy to make Tempest the desirable band it is, yet he tells me all this? Why not plan his schemes with Dax or Nate or, hell, you? You're the master manipulator, right?"

She hears this like it's a compliment. "So you're just leading Abby on because Eddie told you to? Wow...I'm impressed. She has no idea."

"Because I'm not. I'm not leading her on." I take the last shot as I think of my next words. "At first, I was just going to bang her. But then I was...drawn to her. She feels it too. And Eddie...then Eddie tells me he needs her to fall for a band member to ensure her loyalty, and—but—at that point, it was already happening, you know?" No need to trick her into falling in love with anyone when I'd already fallen hard. Shit. I've fallen hard. I want her, and it's not just about the sex. This revelation is terrifying, yet I need her. I need to be with her. Now.

I barely acknowledge Ken's still sitting across from me. She's mumbling on about something, but I only catch the tail end of it, "...then you should be with her."

She's got that right. With a newfound determination, I decide I'm going back to the hotel room to tell Abby everything. She deserves to know how I feel. I push myself up to standing and immediately fall on my ass. Drunk and high, my mood's definitely been lifted, but I'm too wasted to move.

Kennedy's standing over me, laughing. "Need some help?"

She offers a hand and gets me back to standing. Now we're both laughing. See, she's not so bad. "Come on," she says. "I'll find someone who can escort you back to the room safely."

Cloudy vision and weak legs, I stumble with Ken back into the party. She stops me at a group of people, and at this point my eyes are too heavy to keep open. Fuck, I drank too much. Abby's not going to like this.

"Room 803. Make sure he gets into a bed and keep an eye on him until I get back. We need him sober and safe in the morning."

Hands wrap around my arms and I'm floating away, out a door, down a hall, into an elevator. Surreal. Like a dream. Where's Abby? I want to talk to her. I want her to know what she means to me. I want... I want... to sleep.

Chapter Eight

Abby

"You need to eat something," I tell Allie. She's puked twice since we got back to the room. Now she's splayed out diagonally across the bed, her hands covering her face. "Stay right here. I'll be back in a minute."

I go out to the kitchen hoping it's been stocked with something. I find a loaf of bread and some butter in the refrigerator, so toast it is. I feel bad for Allie, but this doesn't surprise me at all. Sex and alcohol have been her vices for so long. Once she had the baby, she toned it down a little, but this was her first night out in a long time. I should've known she'd let loose and go overboard. And what was I doing while she was downing drink after drink? Oh right, screwing around with Miles. I smile, realizing how Allie and I are probably more alike than either of us know.

I finish making her toast and put it on a plate, ready to bring it to her, when I hear the lock on our door beep. The sounds of heavy feet and giggling fill the empty space, and I assume it's Nate coming back with tonight's picks. These rock stars definitely do lead extraordinary lives. I take a peek out of the kitchen to see how many he's brought back tonight.

And I nearly drop the glass plate. It's not Nate.

It's Miles.

And to answer my question, it's two women he's brought back. One in a very short green skirt with her ass hanging out. The other in a backless top. They cling to Miles like glue as they all hobble through the living room.

The three of them go to the nearest bedroom, and when the door closes behind him, my stomach flips. I'm seconds away from being sick, yet I'm frozen in place.

How could he do this?

Did he think I wouldn't find out?

Was he planning on lying to me about it?

I was so sure he was a different guy with me—that I brought out the man he wanted to be. Dammit. I try to think back to the past several nights. Was he with me all night? Can I think of any time he had to go somewhere and leave me? Like tonight, with the missed calls and Eddie. Maybe Eddie was a cover. Maybe he had sex with me and then immediately went off to find more.

"Abby?" Allie calls from our room, groaning.

I take the plate and hurry in there, afraid of anyone coming out of Miles's room. I'm not ready to talk to him about this. What do I do? What do I say?

I close the door behind me and try to conceal my shock.

"You're the best, you know?"

Allie's trying to sit up in bed. I hand her the food. "Here. Eat this. Then get some sleep. You'll feel better in the morning."

I sit on the edge of the bed, facing away from Allie. She can't see me like this right now. My eyes are burning as I fight back tears, so I let them fall, silently.

"Kudos to you for sticking up to that bitch, by the way. I didn't know you had it in you to punch somebody."

I shake my head. "I smacked her. Like a schoolgirl. It was pathetic." But I really could punch something—or somebody—right now. What was going on in that room? By now, the three of them are probably naked, Miles getting more from those sluts than he could get from me alone.

"You okay?" Allie asks.

I slow my breathing, trying to steady my shaking. "I'm fine," I blurt out. I'm not fine. Not at all.

"I'm sorry." I hear her bite into the toast. She sounds better already. "That stuff I said about Miles. I shouldn't have jumped to conclusions. You say he's a good guy. I'm sure he's a good guy."

I can't hear this right now.

She doesn't stop though. "I'm happy you found someone you really like. You deserve it."

It's too much. Now I know I'm going to be sick. My throat catches and my stomach jolts. I jump off the bed and race into the bathroom just in time.

*

The next morning, I'm sitting at the bar in the kitchen cupping a mug of coffee in my hands. The heat hurts my palms, but everything else hurts worse. I couldn't sleep. Allie was passed out by the time I came out of the bathroom. For hours, I tossed and turned in bed, trying to fall asleep, but every time I closed my eyes I saw Miles. And I saw those women.

What did they have that I didn't? I thought he wanted more than some meaningless fling.

The tears threaten to return, and I take a deep breath, pushing it all away. I refuse to act like some victim. That's why I'm sitting here. Livid, I'm waiting for Miles to make an appearance, and I'm planning on making him explain himself. He might have gotten away with this kind of stuff with others, but it's not going to be okay with me. He's going to tell me why he did this, and then...and then I'm going to leave. Allie was right. I do deserve someone I really care about, but I also deserve someone who feels the same about me. And Miles—

A door opens and my heart stops. It's not his room though. Thank god. I'm not ready for this confrontation. Not that I'll be ready when it does happen.

"Hey." It's Kennedy and she takes a seat next to me. "You all right?"

I'm not looking at her but staring toward Miles's door. "No," I say, bluntly.

She sees where I'm looking and nods her head slowly. "Oh." She lowers her voice like anyone's around to hear. "Did he mess things up?"

To put it lightly.

"I don't want to talk about it."

Kennedy doesn't take a hint and turns to face me. "Listen, I'm sorry. Sorry about last night, and sorry about Miles."

She's waiting for a response, but I have nothing to say to her.

"I understand you're mad," she says, "at me and Miles. You have every right. But you have to know everything I did was to protect you."

"Protect me?" Is she out of her mind? She's been nothing but cruel to me. She doesn't care about my well-being.

"I know. I'm not very good at it, but I knew something like this would happen. It's just the way Miles is. He doesn't do serious relation-ships, and I think that's what you were hop-ing for. Yeah, a part of me wanted to protect my brother too. He's been hurt before, but you're a sweet girl, and I knew he'd hurt you worse."

Wow. For the first time, Kennedy's mak-ing sense. What sort of twilight zone have I entered?

"There's one more thing you should know."

Great, because all I want is more bad news. "Kennedy, I don't—"

"Hear me out, please. You have a right to know this."

"What?" If anything, she's good at raising suspense.

"Miles was leading you on."

No crap. "That seems to be obvious."

"No. He was doing it because of Eddie. Eddie told him to seduce you. To make you fall for him."

"And why would he do that?" Never mind the knife that's twisting in my heart right now.

"To keep you on our side. I'm sure you would've found out either way, so I knew it was better coming from me. Eddie wanted to guarantee a positive story out of you, so he told Miles to make you fall for him."

My eyes fill with tears again, and this time I can't control it. I wipe at my face, feeling like a fool.

Kennedy puts her hand on my shoulder. As much as I don't like her, at least someone around here can tell the truth.

"Let me know how I can help," she offers. "But please, when you do write your article, don't let your personal feelings get in the way of good journalism. Any tabloid can throw us under the bus. I really hope you don't decide to do the same."

So that's why she told me. She's worried I'll ruin the whole band because of Miles. The thought hadn't occurred to me. Then again, nothing about my job was anywhere in my thoughts at this point. But it would be a hell of a way to get back at Miles for betraying me.

He cheated on me. He led me on. He was lying the whole time. I can't grasp all this right now.

I have to get out of here.

I get up and go to my room where Allie's still asleep. Nudging her shoulder, I wake her up. "Allie. I need you to get up."

Groggy, she rolls over and rubs at her eyes. "What time is it?"

"Earlier than you like, but we have to go."

This wakes her up. She struggles to sit up, grasping at her head. I imagine her hangover really sucks. "What's wrong?"

"I'll tell you in the car. Get dressed. I'll drive."

She slowly stands up, moving toward the bathroom door, yawning. "Where are we going?"

The only place I can bear to be right now. "Home."

Chapter Nine

Miles

The piercing sunlight feels like a thousand daggers digging into my skull. I try to block out the sun with a pillow, but the extra space all around me brings me out of my half-asleep state. I'm alone in bed. That's unusual.

I roll over and survey the room, everything looking foreign to me. Damn. It's been a long time since I've had a hangover like this. Sitting up, I clutch my forehead in my hand and look around for anything familiar.

Over there. My bag.

Good. At least I'm in the right hotel room. But where's Abby? Maybe she's out there being amazing and making me a hangover breakfast. I could really use an omelet. I smile at the mere thought of her taking care of me. Yep, I've definitely fallen hard. I want to wake up to that woman every morning.

Hobbling out of bed, I find my jeans in a crumpled pile on the floor and put them on. Skipping the shirt, I go in the bathroom to give myself a quick once over. Damn. I look like I feel. After splashing some water on my face, I push my hair out of my eyes and brush my teeth. There, now I'm more approachable.

As soon as I leave the room, I sense something is off. Maybe because I was expecting Abby to be out here. Or maybe because the only one up is Kennedy, and it looks like she's sitting in that chair over there waiting for me.

"Good morning, stud," she says, an evil smile on her face. "Glad to see you're back to your old self."

"What the hell's that supposed to mean?" I go into the kitchen and pour a cup of coffee before locating a frying pan. If Abby's not making me breakfast, then I'll just surprise her by cooking for her instead.

"It means, Old Miles has returned. At least, that's what I assume by the two women doing their walk of shame out of your room a couple hours ago."

I can't stop the pan from falling. It clatters to the ground with a loud bang. No, no, no. I was alone in there. I would've been able to tell if I'd slept with another—*two other*—women. "Don't bullshit me," I tell Kennedy, retrieving the pan and finding some eggs in the fridge.

She gets up and joins me in the kitchen. "You tell me, then. What do you remember from last night?"

"I remember having sex with Abby."

"Please, spare me the details," she whines, sitting down at the bar, waiting for me to continue.

"I remember Eddie being a pain in my ass. And I remember—" I fight with my brain to replay the events of last night. "I remember..." Shit. Nothing. Nothing's coming back to me.

"See what I mean? Unfortunately, your girlfriend was much less drunk and watched you come back with a couple of groupies. And you all weren't exactly quiet. She probably was awake listening all night, and then this morning...when they left. She was right here."

"I would never do that to her. You're fucking with me." She has to be lying. I don't care how trashed I was last night, I can control myself.

"I wish I was. Instead, I was the one trying to comfort her this morning. She left, Miles."

I shake my head. "Stop your games, Ken."

"See for yourself." She points to one of the other rooms. "That's where she and her sister were last night."

I storm into the room, hoping I'd catch Abby coming out of the shower or something. But it's empty. All of Abby's things are gone.

Kennedy fills in the blanks. "She left with her sister. I guess small town girl couldn't handle the big times. She went home."

"What the fuck happened, Kennedy?" I'm yelling now, ready to punch my fist through a wall.

"What happened was, I was right. I've been right all along. You were blinded by your own delusions, destined to revert back to your old ways. Suck it up."

"I wouldn't hurt her like that." I leave the room intending to go back to mine, get dressed, and go find Abby.

"Oh, but you didn't."

I stop in my tracks and swing back around toward Kennedy.

"You didn't hurt her, Miles. I was right on that part too. She was using you to get the information she needed. When she left this morning, she seemed...satisfied. Even told her sister she needed to get out of here, away from us, so she could write her little story. While you were playing Romeo, she was snooping around. And I guess she found what she was looking for. Your slutty act last night just made it easier for her to sever ties. She doesn't care about you, big bro. She never did."

The nearest thing to me is the couch. I fall into the back of it, letting it support me. I shake my head, but I have no words.

Kennedy comes over and hugs me. "I'm sorry. I really am." She straightens back up, looking me dead in the eye. "I think she found out the whole truth about you. Whatever she decides to do with it... Well, you can't say I didn't warn you."

* * *

Abby

It's hard to drive and cry at the same time, so we never made it out of Dallas. We stopped at a coffee shop for Allie and have been sitting here for nearly two hours. I told her everything. How my feelings for Miles grew beyond my control, how Kennedy threatened me, how Miles is full of mystery but showed me a different side of him. How it was all a lie. I even told her about *ScandalLust's* offer and how I refused to betray him. Funny how that turned around and bit me on the ass.

"How can he act like that with me just to lead me on?" I stare at my styrofoam coffee cup as if it'll answer me.

"Maybe being a manipulator runs in his family. I mean, all the time he and Kennedy spend together...you never know."

"I can't believe that. It doesn't make sense." Explain the song he wrote. Explain the look in his eyes when he was lusting for me, completely vulnerable to me. There was nothing fake in that. "I just want answers."

"You want to go back and talk to him?"

The thought terrifies me. "No. Not yet. If I matter to him at all, he can come to me." And I want time to convince myself it's all one big misunderstanding. It wouldn't be the first time Kennedy lied to me. But that doesn't explain the women hanging on Miles. No...that's on him.

"Well, we can't just sit here." Allie gets up and pulls me to standing, embracing me in a big hug. "Let's think up something to do on a Friday afternoon in Dallas."

A brief memory flashes across my mind. There was something to do this afternoon. But it wasn't on my schedule. It was on Miles's. "We could stake out Frankie's Diner and see who Miles was secretly meeting with at one o'clock?"

"Perfect!" she says.

"I was joking. I'm not a crazy person."

She laughs and tugs me toward the door. "No," she looks down at her watch, "but I am."

Allie drives this time as I sit in the passenger seat insisting we not do this. "All it takes is one paparazzi jerk to see us and I'm labeled a psycho stalker forever."

"No one will see. Besides, who's to say we didn't have our own errands to run and just happened to be in the same place at the same time?"

"It's a bad idea." But I don't fight with her over it. A part of me is curious. Another part is certain this will amount to nothing.

"You wanted answers. I'm going to help you get some."

*

We parallel park across the street from Frankie's, and I say a silent prayer of thanks that Allie's car is as generic as they come. I check the clock. 12:53. My heart thumps loudly, and I kind of hope Miles doesn't show up. But as soon as I think it, I spot him across the street walking down the sidewalk.

"There he is," I whisper.

Allie laughs at me. "What? You think he'll hear you?"

"Shut up."

We sit in silence as he waltzes toward Frankie's with an air of confidence. My heart twists. He was deceiving me. A man I thought I could really love...was lying to me. Seeing him brings up a mix of feelings—lust, fear, disappointment, yearning. How did it all go wrong so quick? As he reaches the door, he looks over his shoulder, a fleeting expression of concern on his face. He's worried he was followed. What's he doing right now that he doesn't want to be caught?

"I can barely see him through those windows. Let's get a closer look." Allie opens her door to get out, but I yank her back in.

"No way in hell. This is already sneaky enough. We are not following him...more than we already have."

She relents and closes her door. Now we're both staring toward the oversized windows of Frankie's. I can make out a few tables and chairs. Occasionally, a waitress walks close enough to the windows to see they wear dark red aprons. And I can just barely make out Miles's silhouette as he sits down across from another silhouette. I squint my eyes to try and focus. Who's he with? But it's no use. I can only tell it's Miles. That same waitress walks by their table and sets down a couple glasses. For a second, Miles turns to face her, and I can tell from his profile he's smiling. My heart flutters. I want that sexy smile to be aimed at me again.

But it's too late.

"What's he doing?" Allie asks.

"I'm not sure. Reading a menu?"

"Is this a secret lunch date?"

"I hope not."

We wait a little longer until it feels like we're going nowhere with this. Allie's still excited about being a detective, but I'm feeling more guilty by the second. We shouldn't be here.

"Let's just go." No way can I sit here through the rendezvous with his mystery date.

Allie starts the car and pulls out of the spot. She glances toward the diner one last time. "He's doing something." She squints, trying to see clearer.

"Eating?"

"No, smart ass. He's...signing something."

A car honks behind us, forcing us to get moving before we can see anything more.

Chapter Ten

Miles

"This should cover the next six months." I scrawl my signature across the bottom of the check and slide it across the table. "So things are still fine, right?"

I look up, waiting for Eddie to respond. After last night and this morning, it feels like everything can come undone at any second.

"Yeah. Things are fine," he says, pocketing my check and returning to his lunch. "As long as you tone down the rock star antics."

Even I can admit last night was too much. Eddie's around to watch my back. I shouldn't go making it harder on him. "Don't worry about it." I try to sound reassuring.

"It's my job to worry. You know how lucky you are to have me around, but you have to keep a level head if you don't want to screw it up."

Do I bother mentioning how screwed up everything already is? "I know. I'm sorry."

"That's a start. But guns, public intoxication, drugs...all that shit is going to land you in the same place if you don't watch it."

"I don't need the lecture right now, man."

"You're getting it either way. Stop your shit and stay focused on the big picture." He lowers his voice and looks around the diner, making sure no one's paying too close of attention. "You know where I need you to be Monday night, right?"

I sigh. Not this again, but it's a sort of commitment I can't get out of. "Is it all set up?"

"Of course. I took care of everything."

"I was just hoping we could reschedule or—"

He lets out a guffaw. "This isn't something you simply *reschedule*, Miles. You know what happens if you don't do your part."

"Fine. I get it. I'll be there."

We eat in silence for a few minutes, but I really don't feel like eating.

"Tell me about the reporter. Things good with her?"

There goes the rest of my appetite. There's no way I can tell him Abby knows everything. He'd flip a shit right here, but he's going to notice she's not around.

"Not exactly," I confess. "I screwed up. She left this morning."

"Perfect." He drops his fork onto his plate. "Fucking perfect. We have to get on the road, and she needs to be on that bus."

"She's gone, Eddie. We'll have to deal with whatever happens as it comes."

"You're just going to roll over and die like that? You're a quitter? We're doing all this to protect *you*, Miles. We can just as easily kick you out of the band and let you deal with your own consequences. Instead, you put your band members at risk. You put me at risk. And all I needed was for you to do this one thing. Make Abby fall for you. Period. It was going fine, judging by your public display last night at the party. So if you fucked things up between then and now, your ass is going to fix it."

"Eddie, I—"

"It's not up for discussion." He grabs his wallet and throws cash onto the table before storming out of the diner.

Trust me, man. I'd love to fix it. But I don't even know what happened.

*

When I get back to the hotel, everyone's packing up to head down to Austin. I have no idea how or when I'm supposed to track Abby down when I have to be on the road today, have a show tomorrow, and have no idea where her family lives anyway.

I go into my room to pack my stuff but end up collapsing on the bed instead.

Why'd I have to fall for her? This would be much simpler if I'd spared my own feelings, if I'd guarded myself the way I used to. Then I wouldn't care about fixing things.

But even if I didn't care, I *had* to do something. Eddie was right. We need her on our side, and if she's really figured out the truth, she can drag us down faster than a crashing plane. So am I doing this for him? For the band? Or for myself?

A soft knock on my door is followed by Kennedy's head peeking in. "How are you doing?" she asks with a sincere voice.

Something inside my head clicks. This isn't normal Kennedy. She loves a good "I told you so", but her acting affectionate and sweet...I know that's fake.

"What did you say to Abby?"

She comes further into the room and closes the door. "What do you mean?" The innocence in her voice makes me nauseous.

"I didn't fuck those girls last night. Whether I remember it or not, I know I didn't. And there's no way she could've found out the real truth. Not unless you said something. The only people who know are you, me, and Eddie, and I know Eddie isn't talking."

"Whatever, Miles. I didn't say anything." She leaves the room, but I follow her. Everyone—Dax, Nate, even Devon—is crowded into the living room ready to go back to the tour bus. Awesome, an audience. Just what I need.

"Don't fucking lie to me, Kennedy."

She spins around and points an angry finger at me. "Fuck you, Miles." I see Devon get up like he's going to step in between us. Not sure who he thinks he's protecting in the process. "Maybe you made some deep confession while you were trashed," Kennedy says.

"How could I have if I was supposedly in here screwing a couple groupies?" I'm inches from her face now, my fists clenched at my side.

"Is there a problem here?" Devon asks.

"Yeah." Everyone's eyes are on us now, but I don't care. They can all hear this. "Your girlfriend is trying to ruin everything that matters to me." I glare at my sister, the great puppetmaster. "You had something to do with this. I'm sure of it. And I'm going to figure it out."

* * *

Abby

My heart seems to stop when we pull into the only home I've ever known. It's been awhile since I've visited, yet it's all so comfortably familiar. The white paint fading on the wrap-around porch, the poplar tree blossoming in the side of the yard. And when we get inside, the smell really brings me back. Clean cotton sheets and the smells of vanilla and cinnamon coming from the kitchen. My mom always loved to bake, especially when we were in a bad mood. She'd make up a cobbler or a batch of muffins, and we'd sit at the table spilling our guts to her.

I smile. Allie must have clued her in that we were coming.

"My girls!" I hear my mom shout from the kitchen. She rushes out and embraces us both at the same time, kissing the tops of our heads. It doesn't matter if we were gone for a day—like Allie—or half a year—like me. She always made us feel missed and appreciated. It was good to be home.

"Whatcha cooking?" Allie asks.

"Abby's favorite pick-me-up."

"Cinnamon rolls," I answer for her. Of course.

And just like that, I feel safe and content—
the outside world unable to bother me when
I'm in here. Mom finishes baking while I drop
my things off in my old room. It's like a time
capsule of my past, still looking just how I left
it. The same old books on the shelves, my
childhood stuffed lion on the rocking chair in
the corner, my first guitar hanging on its
hook next to my bed. I shake my head in dis-
belief. It really feels like I've gone back in
time.

That is, until my ringing phone reminds
me I'm in the present. It's a text from Dee.

Hello, woman. Need an update. Video chat?

I dig my laptop out of my bag and plug it
in. Settling onto my old bed, I make a video
chat request.

"There you are," is how she answers. Then
she notices the things behind me. "Wait.
Where are you exactly?"

I look back over my shoulder. Yeah, I suppose a decade-old beach scene poster isn't
what you'd typically find on a tour bus or in a

fancy hotel. But I'm not in the mood to explain everything for the second time today, so I lie...

"I took advantage of being near my old childhood home to come and visit for the night."

"Aww," she says. Then she puts on an exaggerated Southern accent. "Did you bring the boyfriend home to meet your mom?" She grins wildly while a rock forms in my throat.

"Um...no. Not this time." Or any time in the future for that matter.

The view on the screen shifts, and I see my sweet golden retriever leap into view.

Dee laughs. "I think he recognized your voice."

"Hi Chord!" I shout to him as though he really has any clue how to video chat with me, but seeing him proves to be too much and my eyes run over with tears.

Dee notices fast. "Honey, what's wrong?"

I dry my face and shake my head, rolling my eyes at my own stupidity. "Nothing. Just homesick, I guess."

"You'll be back soon. Your week's almost up, right?"

It is. I hadn't even thought of that. No matter where Miles and I stand, I leave in a couple days. Certainly, the distance will drive us even further apart, and soon enough, he'll forget about me in favor of going back to his one-woman-a-night lifestyle. The thought makes me sick.

"So have you thought more about your *ScandalLust* predicament?"

It's the last thing on my mind right now, but hey, maybe this newest drama can make me fifty grand. I wonder if they'd care about a story about their rock star sex symbol breaking hearts. Or maybe something about Kennedy sneaking around behind Devon's back—not that I have any proof she is. But...

"No, I'm completely incapable of being an asshole."

"Whoa there, Spunky. It's a good thing, remember? Having integrity... Not screwing over your boyfriend."

But he's not my boyfriend. I almost confess everything, but it's easier to run away from my problems right now than it is to deal with them.

"Yeah. Listen. I need to go. My mom's waiting for me downstairs." It's not exactly a lie. I told her I'd be back down quickly.

We say our goodbyes and I get one more glimpse of Chord. I miss my apartment. And my friend. And my dog...

And a level of normal I don't think I'll ever be able to experience again. Was it worth it? I don't know. I can't answer that right now. At least I'll be back home soon. This assignment will be behind me, and I can take control of my own life again.

Chapter Eleven

Abby

Everything feels foreign when I wake up the next morning. Sure, I'm in the comfort of my old bed in my old room, but that's just it. I'd gotten so used to thrill and excitement, even the chaos of living in Los Angeles, that to be somewhere so...safe...seems unreal.

"Abby," my mom calls from downstairs.

I try to catch the scent of what's for breakfast, but all I smell is the fresh detergent smell of the quilt wrapped around me. I stumble out of bed, wearing pajama pants and a tank top, and work my way downstairs.

"Good morning," I'm prepared to say when I enter the kitchen, but my voice catches the second I walk in.

It would've been unsurprising to see Allie in here with my mom. She lives nearby and would happily extend her visit with me by showing up for breakfast. I would've been less surprised to find my extended family. After all, it'd been a long time since I last visited.

But when I walk into the kitchen, and find my mother sitting across from Kennedy Rose and Devon Stone, it's like two worlds colliding, and my universe can't handle it.

"How'd you find me?" I demand, clearly unpleased about their unwelcome visit.

"I have contacts," Devon says. "Kennedy needs to talk to you." He sounds pissed off.

I look from him to Kennedy to my mom.

"Oh, you girls can go in the living room and talk. I'll keep Mr. Tall and Handsome here company." She turns to Devon. "You like eggs? I can make some eggs."

This is not happening. Devon graciously accepts like he's a friggin boy next door while Kennedy gets up from the table and walks past me.

"You have no right to be here," I blurt out, too shocked to care about kindness.

"I wouldn't be, but Devon insisted." She takes a seat on the couch, but I remain standing, my arms crossed in front of my chest. "Listen. The shit with Miles—"

"I don't want more excuses. I'm sick of being lied to."

"He didn't sleep with those women. He was trashed and I told them to help him back to the room."

What the hell? "But you were the one there to comfort me. This is just some twisted game to you?"

"Not exactly." Her choice of words makes me want to wring her neck. "There's a lot of bad history between me and Miles. He'd always interfere with my life, so I interfered with his."

"Oh, so it's that simple? You screwed with our relationship in order to get revenge. How old are you?"

"Hold on, bitch. I still don't think you're good for him, but I'll let you two figure it out the hard way."

"Then why'd you come here in the first place? To apologize and then insult me?"

"Have you heard me utter an apology? I'm far from sorry." She sighs. "But apparently *my boyfriend* made some truce with Miles. So when he saw me and Miles fighting, and found out why, he made me come here and make things right."

Unbelievable. Devon Stone to the rescue? "So it was all a lie you made up? Miles cheating? Miles leading me on? The stuff about Eddie?"

She stays silent too long. "Most of it, yeah."

"Then what part of it is true?"

"I had nothing to do with the Eddie stuff. You'll have to talk to your boyfriend about that."

"But what do you know about it? You knew enough to tell me. What parts *didn't* come from your deranged mind?" I lean against the chair. The little hope I had that it was all a mistake has since vanished.

"Miles told me about the stuff with Eddie. That's all I've got. I didn't embellish."

"So his feelings were never real anyway." Perfect. Thanks for clearing that up, Kennedy. I feel *so* much better. "You've done what you came here to do. I think it's time for you to leave."

"How much do you know about Miles?"

Her question catches me off guard.

"Not as much as I'd like to know." She needs to take a hint and leave.

"But did he tell you anything? Anything you probably shouldn't have known?"

What is she talking about? We'd hardly had the chance to tell each other our deepest secrets. "Like what?"

"Like something *ScandalLust* would like to know?"

My heart jolts at the mention of that stupid tabloid.

Kennedy sees the shock in my face. "What did you tell *ScandalLust*? I know you're working with them. You try to act all sweet and innocent, but you're just as manipulative as I am."

"I'm *not* working with *ScandalLust,* and that's the last time you'll ever compare me to yourself." I almost remind her I want her out of my house, but then I find myself with more questions. "What's so bad about Miles that you're worried I know? If we're together, don't you think I'll find out anyway?"

"Not if he knows what's good for him."

"What's that supposed to mean?"

"It means he has to keep his mouth shut. If word gets out, it can ruin all of us. And I promise you, if my life gets screwed up because of your snooping, I'll make sure you both live to regret it."

What can possibly be such a big deal that she's got to throw more threats at me? "What is it? The drugs? The promiscuity?"

She lets out a guffaw. "That's not even newsworthy. Let me just repeat myself. Your life would be better without Miles. Trust me."

"Trust you? Right. You've really proven you care. Thanks again, Kennedy. You've been so incredibly helpful."

Instead of seeing my guests out, I head back upstairs and slam the door behind me. A few minutes later, I hear the front door close. Out my window, I see Kennedy and Devon get back into their car and their driver pull away.

I could fall back to sleep and dream away this nightmare, but a knock on my door tells me it's not an option. My mom comes in.

"Come downstairs and eat something."

"I'm not hungry," I tell her.

"Tough. Eat anyway. And while you're down there, you're going to tell me why those Hollywood people showed up at my door."

* * *

Miles

The drive from Dallas to Austin was the shortest yet, but it felt like it took forever. Abby leaving has created a noticeable absence that no amount of liquor can fix. Now I'm supposed to stand on a stage and play to a crowd of strangers. I don't have time for this. I have to fix things. Not because Eddie said so, but because I *need* to. I *need* Abby.

Backstage, I screw with the tuning on my guitar waiting for the opening band to finish. I've been avoiding everyone else, my mind in a completely different place.

I feel a hand slap me in the back, and I whirl around defensively.

"Lighten up, brother." It's Kennedy. I've hardly seen her at all today. I was counting on her staying far from me while I deal with her latest nonsense. Instead, she's back in my face, this time handing me a piece of paper. "You might want this."

I look down at the scrawled letters printed on a torn sticky note. It's an address.

"What is this? The postal address to hell? Funny, I thought I was already there."

"Hilarious, comedian. It's Abby's house. Her mom's place. That's where she's staying."

I shove it into my pocket. "And why would you give it to me? How'd you even find it?"

"Devon helped. He brought me there today—"

"Wait. You saw her? The last thing I need is for you to go around screwing things up worse."

"I went to tell her the truth. That you didn't cheat on her." She takes a step back like it's the end of the conversation. "But the rest of it is all on you. If you want her back, you have to fix it."

*

Midway through our set, I know I'm sucking. Fortunately, the crowd hasn't caught on, but not only did I start playing the wrong intro to our third song, but I've been making Kennedy pull all the weight on vocals, barely singing my parts. The whole place is a blur to me, and as we near the end, my heartbeat starts to race.

The second we finish, I know exactly what I have to do.

"What the hell, man?" Dax stops me back-stage. "Where were you tonight?"

"Don't worry about it."

"Oh right. I won't worry about it. We can just suck and then kiss our contract goodbye. Sounds about right."

I shove him backward, not in the mood to be criticized right now. "I'm going through some shit right now. Got it? Now back off."

Without waiting for a response, I push past him and leave the venue. Eddie's out back, smoking a cigarette.

"Hey," he shouts at me as I rush past him.

"Not now."

"You okay?" he asks. "It's not like you to have such an off night."

I spin around, ready to fight with him too. "I wouldn't have an off night if it weren't for you."

"I'm pretty sure I wasn't the one on that stage tonight."

"No. But you were the one to insist on bringing a reporter on tour. And you're the one who told me we had to keep her close. And now things are fucked up."

"And I told you to fix them. Where is she, anyway?"

"Not here. But I'm going to find her." I turn to leave, but realize Eddie could be of use. "I need your keys." I hold out my hand to him.

"Like hell." He drops his cigarette and stomps on it.

"You want me to fix things. Lend me your car. I'll fix them."

He relents and digs his keys out of his pocket. "A single scratch, and your relation-ship problems will be the least of your concerns."

Ignoring him, I walk off and find his Benz parked behind our bus. I'm not sure what I'm going to do yet, but I've got over an hour's drive to figure it out.

Chapter Twelve

Miles

Dirt roads and one-light towns lead me to Abby's childhood home. I pull up quietly, immediately noticing her on the front porch. She's sitting in a rocking chair with a baby in her arms. Must be her sister's kid. On the other side of the porch, I spot her sister, sitting at a table, playing a card game with an older woman—their mom, I presume.

Well, I wasn't planning on making a show in front of the whole family, but if that's what it takes to win her back, so be it. When I get out of the car, the sudden quiet is startling. Instead of bright lights and glowing billboards, the sky is pitch black and sprinkled with stars. Instead of the sounds of traffic and hectic nightlife, I hear crickets and a soft voice singing.

I walk up the driveway and listen to the soothing voice singing a lullaby. It's Abby singing. And she sounds beautiful. Dammit. Why'd I have to screw everything up?

The second I tap on the screen door, she stops singing and looks up. Our eyes meet and it takes a second before either of us can speak.

"Miles." She stops rocking the chair, and I see the baby stir in his sleep.

"Sorry," I say. *For everything. I'm such an asshole and you're better off without me.* "Sorry for showing up so late."

She stands up and brings the baby to Allie, then comes to the door and holds it open for me. "We need to talk."

I smile. "That's what I was going to say."

She leads me into the house, and I'm blown away by how comfortable it is. Family photos on the wall, warm colors everywhere, pleasant smells from home-cooked meals. This is everything I never had growing up. I look at the nearest wall, at the collage of photos covering it. It's easy to spot Abby, her curly blond hair and bright, excited eyes. There are photos of her playing with a dog in the yard. Another hugging a man, her dad maybe? There's a photo clearly from prom where she's decked out in a red dress with too much makeup. Her date's some kid with a buzz cut, smiling like an idiot. I bet that guy knew how lucky he was. Meanwhile, I'm the real screw up.

"Abby, I'm sorry. About everything."

"Kennedy came over this morning. She confessed to lying about you and those women. I'm surprised she's even capable of telling the truth."

I laugh. "I know what you mean. I don't know what her problem is, but—"

"That's not what we need to talk about." She interrupts me, and it's clear she's angry with me. "I don't care about Kennedy. I care about you. And all the lies you've been feeding me." She drops down into a chair and hides her face in her hands. When she looks back up, she's more tired than sad.

"You just said Kennedy came by to clear everything up." I'm confused. What more can I do when I wasn't the bad guy to begin with?

"Yeah. She cleared things up about the groupies. Said she sent them on purpose, and all they did was make sure you made it to your room. Now you can explain the rest."

"What rest? That's it."

"You have nothing else you've been keeping from me?"

My memory jumps back to Kennedy telling me Abby knows everything. Is it true? If so, then she deserves my side of the story. But if it's not...I can't risk ratting myself out, especially not with us on such shaky ground right now.

"Abby, I haven't lied to you. Everything that's happened between us, my feelings, it's all genuine."

"So, no secrets then?"

"No. I mean...we don't know each other yet. There's still a lot to learn. But I haven't been lying to you." That's mostly the truth. The only thing I've kept from her is the thing I've kept from everyone. But I'm not the only one guilty of keeping secrets. "What about you?"

"Me?" She still seems angry. What else does she know?

"Care to tell me what *your* real intentions are?" Is this why she's digging for secrets? Trying to finish her deal with *ScandalLust*?

"How can you turn this on me? I've been the pawn in some absurd game. I was only supposed to be here to do my job. Then everything else happened. You and me and—"

"And *ScandalLust*?"

She freezes, her eyes glaring at me. Her silence is like a scream.

"I know you're working with them."

"How could you—Who—"

"Kennedy has a tendency to be very...observant."

She shakes her head, her face filled with disgust. "So she was snooping."

"No worse than you, apparently."

Abby stands up, tall, prepared to go on the defense. "Miles, it's nothing. I—"

"Why didn't you just tell me sooner if it was nothing?"

"They were offering me a deal. Fifty-thousand dollars in exchange for inside information. But it doesn't matter. Besides, if you have no secrets from me, then I wouldn't have had anything to sell, right?"

So she's going to play stubborn? "You really would've sold my private information? Unbelievable. This is exactly why I told Eddie not to bring you on tour. You reporters only care about yourselves, is that it? You know? It's fine. You've got nothing on me or my band, so try to make some extra cash. Team up with the fucking tabloids. But this interview is over."

* * *

Abby

How dare he! How dare he really think I'd sacrifice my integrity to work with *Scandal-Lust*. He accuses me of having ulterior motives. What about him? He just lied to my face.

He turns and leaves the house in a rush. No, this isn't over. He's not getting the last word.

I hurry out of the house behind him, rushing out of the porch and down the steps. "Miles!"

He keeps walking.

"Tell your pal, Eddie, I'm sorry his plan didn't work out."

This stops him in his tracks. He turns back to me, the flame in his eyes temporarily extinguished.

"Kennedy told me," I say. "She said Eddie's the one who propositioned you to come after me. You needed me to fall in love with you so that I'd work in your favor. Tell me that's not true."

He doesn't say a word. Movement behind me catches my attention, and I turn in time to see the door close. Mom and Allie went inside, leaving me and Miles to deal with this right in my front yard.

I nod slowly, turning back to Miles. "Yeah. No more secrets, right?"

"You really think I've been lying to you about my feelings? That what we have— *had*—isn't real?"

"I don't know what to think anymore. That's why I'm asking you. I need you to tell me what's real and what isn't. I need you to make all this make sense. I need you to—"

His lips crush into mine, cutting off my words. He tastes me slowly, gently, trying to push thousands of emotions into one long kiss. When he pulls away, I have to catch my breath.

"It's all been real. Eddie did come to me, you're right. He said he needed you attached to one of us to ensure your loyalty."

I don't want to hear any of this. Not when that kiss still lingers on my lips.

He continues, "He had to make sure you'd help us stay in a positive light, and to him, that meant making you fall for one of us. But it was all unnecessary. He didn't need to sit me down or tell me all that, because at that point *I'd* already fallen for *you*. I was never using you. And I really wish you could say the same about me."

"I was never going to work with *Scandal-Lust*. Sure, the money sounded nice, but I'd never do that to you or the band. I wouldn't even do it to Kennedy. But I can't be with you if you can't be honest with me, and she said there's more. She said there's information about you that could ruin everything, and that I'm better off without you. I don't want to be without you. And I can accept if there are secrets you feel you have to keep from me, but as long as those secrets exist, we can't be together."

A tear cascades down my cheek. I'm trying to hold it together, but I'm seconds from collapsing. He's right here in front of me. I can forgive him for everything and forget about the lies. We can go back to how we were. But everything I said is the truth. We can't build a relationship out of dishonesty.

I'm ready to go back inside, curl up in bed, and have a good cry when Miles's shoulders relax. I can see him struggling with his thoughts, and when he looks back at me, his eyes meeting mine, I see the defeat. He doesn't want to let me go.

"Eddie's my probation officer." He inhales deeply. This is obviously hard to confess.

"But he's your manager."

"His first career was in corrections before he started managing. When he was put on my case, it was like a match made in prisoner heaven."

"You were in prison." Ice floods my veins. I never expected this.

"No. It didn't get that far. I—um—I was in another band before Tempest, called His Execution. We were signed to this up-and-coming label, Graffiti Rock Records. They were getting pretty big, pretty fast. Hell, they probably would've been Stone competition at this point."

"Then why are you talking about them in past tense?" I ask. I try not to feel completely uncomfortable right now, but how can I not? My boyfriend—if I can even call him that—is a felon?

"Right after we signed with them, I overheard something I wasn't meant to hear. They were going to exploit us and had plans to take all the money back that we were promised. They'd formed a whole strategy that wouldn't just hurt my band, but the twenty others on the label. I had to do something about it."

Oh no. Please tell me he wasn't arrested for murder. I've seen his temper. He's not afraid to get physical when someone's a threat to him.

"I figured out a way to screw them before they could screw us. I went after every band they had signed. Told them what I'd heard. We started running our tabs up as high as possible. Took extra time in studio to generate extra costs. We'd demand ridiculous, expensive things while playing naive to their intentions. The expenses were certainly hurting them but it wasn't enough." Miles runs his hand through his hair. He almost seems relieved to be telling me all this. But I've yet to find out what the big deal is. "We found a loophole in the contract, and I convinced nine of their signed bands to pull out at the same time. We got a lawyer and everything. It was a battle, but once those nine left the label, Graffiti knew they were fucked. They also realized I was the one behind it. The head of the label showed up at my house and it turned into a big fight. He ended up in the hospital and pressed charges. I went to jail. The label went bankrupt." The corners of his mouth curve into a smile. "It was worth it. Eddie was assigned to my case, and the rest is history."

"So you went to jail for a fight? That's it? I mean, I hate the violence, but that's hardly a big secret to keep from the tabloids. They've seen you fight before."

"It's not about the fight. It's about the power I had over that label. I crushed them. No decent record company is going to want to touch the risk I pose. They can't find out, or we'll never move forward in this business."

It still doesn't make sense to me. "But isn't it public record? Couldn't I look you up right now and see it for myself?"

He shakes his head no. "This is where it helped to have Eddie on our side. He helped me move, start fresh. I went from lead singer to a guitar player in the background. I brought Kennedy in to take the spotlight. And I rebranded myself."

"Rebranded?"

He scrunches his forehead and I get the feeling I'm not going to like this next part. "Miles isn't my real name."

Okay, not as gut punching as I'd expected. Obviously, his last name, Riot, is a stage name, so I guess it's okay that I've only known him as Miles...That I've been sleeping with a man whose name I, technically, didn't know... "What's your real name then?"

He laughs. "Michael Smith. But don't ever tell a soul. It took a lot of effort to blur the link between Michael and Miles, His Execution and Tempest Ultra. Now the connection is practically nonexistent."

It's the Smith that's the most ridiculous. Can his real name be any more...generic? I'm not sure I can picture him as a Michael either. "Your secret's safe with me, *Miles*. So you basically started a new life and there were no consequences?"

"There were plenty of consequences. Besides jail time, I've got another year of probation. One screw up will get me tossed behind bars. I've gotten reamed out by Eddie about my drinking, my temper, smoking pot, even taking you to the range."

I cock my eyebrow. What do I have to do with this?

"I'm not allowed to touch guns," he says plainly.

"So then why break the rules anyway?"

Miles shrugs. "Maybe because I'm an idiot. Or because Eddie lets me get away with more than I should as long as I attend anger management regularly and pay my restitution on time."

Something clicks. "Is that what you were doing—" *at Frankie's Diner yesterday?* I want to say, but that would give away the fact I'd followed him. "Never mind." We saw him signing something. It could've simply been a check if he owes money to his victim. It makes so much sense. "So you have to remain Miles so labels like Stone Records will take a chance with you. If they knew your history, then..."

"We'd never get signed."

"And *ScandalLust* has no idea?"

"Not unless you plan on taking them up on their offer."

I gasp. "I wouldn't—"

"I'm kidding." He steps closer and wraps his arms around my waist. It feels different now that I know who he really is. But different isn't a bad thing. I feel...closer to him. "As long as they're staying on my tail, it's only a matter of time before *ScandalLust* figures it all out. It's a delicate row of dominos right now. If they find out I'm on probation, they'll dig further, and the dominos will fall. They'll find out what happened and they'll tell everybody. That's why you came on tour with us—

to be the *credible* source. To protect us. Now we just need *ScandalLust* to go away."

I try to think of a solution to all this. I want to help. Tempest is so close to hitting it big. They've got two major labels fighting for them. It can't get messed up now. There's got to be something I can do.

"Let me help," I say. Miles waits for me to explain more. "We can come up with a plan to distract *ScandalLust*. I can help you guys buy time."

He looks past me at the house. "So does this mean you and I are okay again?"

I reach around his neck and pull him into a kiss. Judging by the heat that fills me to my core, my feelings for him haven't changed at all. Our lips break free and I settle my head against his chest, breathing in his smell. "That depends on whether or not you'll come in and meet my mom."

Inside, I leave Miles to charm my mother as I run upstairs to grab my things. It's back on tour with Tempest Ultra I go, and this time, I'm much more willing. Funny, a week ago, I was dreading having to step foot on that bus. Now, it's exactly where I belong.

There's a knock on my bedroom door, and I turn to see Allie standing there. "Are things okay with you guys?"

It's a loaded question. Depending on what happens over the next few days, this is merely the calm before the storm, but as for me and Miles... "Yeah, we'll be fine."

Downstairs, my mom is beaming as Miles compliments our Southern home filled with memories. He points out childhood pictures of me and laughs as my mom tells him embarrassing stories I'd rather not be sharing. When Miles spots me, he comes over to carry my bag, tossing it over one of his shoulders. I give mom and Allie hugs. Then I loop my arm around Miles's elbow.

"Okay, rock star. Time to go. We have work to do."

The Lust List

The Lust List - Take Your Pick

They're the world's sexiest bachelors. The men of *ScandalLust* mag's infamous Lust List are young, wealthy, and, oh, did we mention? *Hot*.

When scandal follows them everywhere, there's no hiding from the cameras. They're irresistible, insatiable—and talented in all the right ways. Every woman wants them. But these playboys won't be easy to catch...

The Lust List

Miles Riot

by Mira Bailee

HEART STRINGS
BROKEN STRINGS
STRINGS ATTACHED

AVAILABLE NOW

Acknowledgments

To my family, who supports my wildest dreams; my friends, who think I'm awesome no matter what I do; my editor, Nicole Bailey, who makes all my words much prettier; Najla Qamber, who designs the sexiest book covers; Nova Raines, who took on the challenge of co-authoring this massive series with me; and all my readers, who make this adventure worthwhile—

Thank you.

.

About Mira Bailee

Mira Bailee, a beer-brewing librarian, has been writing leisurely, scholarly, and professionally for the past twenty years.

While she's always maintained a high standard of chaos in her daily routine, *The Lust List* allows her to pass on some of her hectic lifestyle to her characters. Her storytelling balances humor and pleasure with sincerity and conflict, providing a wild ride of human emotions.

In the past she studied filmmaking and screenwriting and determined what goes on behind the scenes is just as tantalizing as what's seen in front of the camera. This revelation is the basis for her inspiration for *The Lust List*.